LIFE'S SEASONS

A COLLECTION OF SHORT STORIES

MALA NAIDOO

Publisher: Independent

First Published in Australia 2019

This edition Published 2019

Copyright © Mala Naidoo 2019

Naidoo, Mala

Life's Seasons — A Collection of Short Stories

ISBN - 978-0-6484854-0-7 (Paperback)

ISBN - 978-06484854-0-21 (Hardback)

ABOUT THE AUTHOR

Mala Naidoo is an Australian author. She was born in South Africa during the apartheid era which is the impetus for her imaginative stories that take on a life of their own when the creative muse beckons. Mala believes that literature speaks through the values and culture of characters, situations and choices, instilling understanding through connections to a moment in time, an event or conversation that brings clarity to daily existence.

ABOUT THE AUTHOR

Mala Naidoo is an Australian author. She was born in South Africa during the apartheid era which is the impetus for her imaginative stories that take on a life of their own when the creative muse beckons. Mala believes that literature speaks through the values and culture of characters, situations and choices, instilling understanding through connections to a moment in time, an event or conversation that brings clarity to daily existence.

ALSO BY MALA NAIDOO

Across Time and Space

Vindication across Time

Souls of Her Daughters

Chosen Lives

What Change May Come

The Rain — A Collection of Short Stories (ebook)

For Billy, lovingly remembered with eternal gratitude for the wisdom and inspiration shared

PART I

LIFE'S SEASONS

Autumn is a second spring when every leaf is a flower
—Albert Camus

ON THE BEACH

Fear hides the truth from yourself

~~~

It was the summer of 1979. A yearly planned holiday after Christmas was here again. Beth packed the land-rover with more food than clothes for an indulgent beach holiday at Pontoon Bay Beach, nestled between two mountains. Except this year Vronegg was reluctant to go, leaving her mother annoyed and confused.

'I don't feel well this morning,' she said, looking at her mother with her big brown, pleading eyes. 'May I please stay with grandma, I don't want to ruin the getaway, Candace and Hazel are keen to have a good time.'

Beth Obrist knew that leaving her daughter with her mother was out of the question — her advancing Alzheimer's would have Vronegg doing as she pleased. She saw it as Neggi's ploy for solitude which she retreated to often this past year. She hated her name and more so hated the multitude of names her mother heaped upon her on a whim, Neggie — Roni — Vroni — and the list went on.

'I'm not feeling well, and please stop calling me 'Neggi,' I will be seventeen next year, and that name sounds like one you would give your pet. Once I can do so, I'm changing my name, why am I 'Vronegg' when I could be Veronica or any other reasonable name?'

'Your father wanted you to have a Swiss name, and I honored his request.'

'What about my request — I never knew him, so what honor does he deserve?'

Beth met Vronegg's father in Switzerland eighteen years ago when she was on a writing research trip. After a whirlwind romance, they married and separated before Vronegg was born. She returned to Australia alone, pregnant and penniless. Meeting Jemima Gutterson was a win for her. They had co-written many books and had a good working relationship. Their friendship strengthened when Jemima's daughters, Candace and Hazel accepted Vronegg more like a sister than friend. This year Beth was going to the beach house alone with the girls, Jemima would join them later in the week.

'I'm sorry, you're not feeling well, take a painkiller and I promise you'll be heaps better before we get to the bay. You can't expect me to go away with Candace and Hazel without you.'

Vronegg shook her head and gave in, her mother had a way of making her feel guilty for being sick or unable to do as she expected. With Beth's writing career, she grew accustomed to being alone when her mother locked herself away from the world, punching out words on her next book. Writing was her obsession. Most of her co-written books were under her own name but a few penned under a different name gave her the anonymity necessary for the sensitivity of her subject matter. Her success as a writer had earned them a comfortable living — the beach house in Pontoon Bay was a luxury they enjoyed. Part of her obsession stemmed from the guilt she carried that Vronegg never knew her father. She would do everything possible to ensure her daughter had a good life.

'Please promise you will stop calling me, Neggi, it's becoming embarrassing around people I meet for the first time. Candace and Hazel call me *Negg* which makes me seem like someone with no identity or some fantastical creation! I'm older now and some of those names are ridiculous!'

'Okay, I get it, now get in the car, I've had three calls from the girls saying they will wait out on the street for us. Let's go!'

Vronegg was striking, her porcelain-white skin and light hair quite opposite to her ruddy-complexioned, dark-haired mother. She looked every bit like her father — the father she never knew and who had since passed away. Her mother reminded her a hundred times over to ensure she had enough sunscreen to protect her pale skin under the harsh sun at Pontoon Bay Beach. They spent most of their days in the water and on the shore, soaking up all they could before they returned to the country with its rolling farmlands, and the nearest neighbor almost five kilometres away. Beth ran her smallholding with four regal stallions, one of them a prime racehorse. The tranquil location gave her the space she needed for uninterrupted writing.

MEMORY of their getaway last year at Pontoon Bay Beach made Vronegg sick to the stomach. She loved Candace and Hazel, but 1978 was a strange summer — one she wanted to forget.

She had blocked recollection of that night out on the beach house balcony, now it was back to claim her peace as the land-rover approached Pontoon Bay. Candace and Hazel were chirpy as ever and dubious about Vronegg being unwell. Fifteen-year-old Hazel leaned across and whispered.

'Are you sick, or lovesick, huh! We heard you and Jaydon have grown close.'

Vronegg would not have her mother on her back about this, she shut her eyes and pretended she was asleep. Eighteen-year-old Candace sat in the front with Beth. She was keen to drive part of the way, but Beth said it was not a good idea with the heavy holiday traffic on the freeway.

'What's made you ill?' Candace asked.

'I'm not sure, but my tummy hurts a lot.'

'Stay away from the corn stand this year, okay!' she laughed.

Vronegg stuck out her tongue in irritation.

All she wanted was to be alone.

THE PONTOON BAY Beach house was an impressive building set in the middle of a cul-de-sac. Five bedrooms, three upstairs overlooking the beach from a large balcony gave the girls a private space while their mothers occupied the bedrooms downstairs. The gap between houses was wide enough to leave curtains and blinds undrawn with no fear of peeking perverts. Rolling sand dunes, a cerulean sky, saltwater air, and waking up to the aroma of bacon and eggs cooking made the break at the bay perfect, except that something had unsettled Vronegg.

1978 STARTED out as a great year, Vronegg was selected to the state basketball team and Beth's horse won the Melbourne Cup making the getaway that summer a special celebration, until one restless night when she went to bed early with tummy cramps, feeling prickly, damp, and queasy. Her mother had cautioned her not to purchase cooked food from random beach vendors. She was pedantic about festering food-bacteria in the Australian summer heat when vendors sold cooked food from an over-packed portable esky on forty degree days.

'I've told you to stay away from the corn stand, those kids don't understand anything about hygiene! Now you've picked up a bug and if it gets worse, I will have to drive you to the hospital! Bacteria breeds in heat and humidity.'

She had heard that mantra many times over the years.

'I'll be fine, I just need to sleep it off.'

Vronegg tossed and turned for most of the night until around midnight — a dreadful burning sensation in her throat forced her to jump up for a drink of chilled water.

Down in the kitchen everything was tidy, whisper-stillness shrouded the cottage. A faint sound of music played somewhere in the distance, the neighbor might have forgotten to turn it off or was awake at that hour.

She was light-headed and in need of air. A breeze blew over from the beach, she stepped out onto the balcony to feel the coolness of the night against her damp skin. She leaned over the balcony to get some blood to her head to stop the dizziness. Across the beach, a low fire was aglow, three figures stood around it. A cover of clouds hid half the moon. Her foggy eyes and darkness made it difficult to discern the age or gender of the figures on the beach. She blinked a few times when one figure stepped away, spun around and lunged at the figure on the same side of the low fire. Two figures rolled on the ground, either in playful or aggressive banter. The figure standing up stepped towards the two on the ground and stepped back in a restless dancing motion, then bent over as if saying something. The constant waltz suggested agitation. Vronegg squinted and squeezed her eyes together to clear her vision. The two stood up and walked away leaving the lone figure circling the low fire. Her tummy churned, she hurried to the bathroom. She returned to the balcony five minutes later — everything was still on the beach. The lone figure was no longer there, the fire was out. All she could see was inky blackness above white, foamy waves crashing on the shore. The urge to walk across to the beach to investigate ended when another bout of nausea hit her. She went back to bed for a few restless hours of sleep, dreaming of the melt-in-your-mouth buttery corn for just a dollar, served by the handsome young man who turned up at the beach in the last three days of their stay. She refused to accept that the delicious barbecued corn had made her unwell. All she could stomach for dinner were a few strawberries, the chops and sausages that her mother had grilled, her favourite, was the last thing she wanted to eat.

SUN STREAMED through the fluttering blinds, the French doors creaked with the heavy winds blowing up to the cottage from the shore. An eruption of police sirens shattered the peacefulness of first light. Candace and Hazel rushed into Vronegg's room.

'There's some commotion out there,' Candace announced.

'Someone left the French doors, open? Who was it?' Hazel looked at Vronegg with accusing eyes.

Candace was quick in denying responsibility. A little voice in Vronegg's head cautioned her to avoid saying anything about last night, 'It must have been the wind, it was gusty in the early hours of the morning.'

They heard Beth call out from downstairs, 'Don't go out on the balcony! Get down here, girls!'

All three stomped down the stairs clad in their flimsy night-wear eager to know what the commotion was.

'So much for a peaceful break with all this rude awakening this early in the day,' Hazel groaned.

Beth's crinkled brow suggested the matter was serious enough for them to pay attention.

'The police have advised that nobody goes down to the beach today. Sorry, ladies we must stay indoors, so find things to entertain yourselves. We have to sit tight until we get further news.'

'What!' Hazel and Candace cried in unison.

Vronegg was silent.

'Why? It's a beautiful day, what's so awful that we can't have a swim this morning?' Hazel peered out the lounge window.

'Get away from the window!' Beth lost her nerve when Hazel lifted the curtain for a better view of the beach. She had taken on the responsibility of coming out to Pontoon Bay with the girls and now she felt an uninvited weight bearing down on her. She had sketchy details on why they could not go down to the beach, but it was enough to exercise caution. Jemima was keen for Hazel and Candace to enjoy their time at the beach this summer without the cloud of her health matters ruining it for them. She never remarried after her husband died. Writing consumed most of her life, and her friendship with Beth was perfect for their little family.

'All I'm appealing for is that we abide by the police's request to remain indoors. It is for our safety.'

'Safety from what? I want to know.' Hazel begged.

Dread claimed the pit of Vronegg's stomach, churning in recollection of what she saw on the beach. She wanted to tell her mother what she had seen that night but thoughts of being questioned by the police halted her. Hazel flicked on the television before Beth could stop her. Breaking news headlines flashed across the screen. Too late, the girl's curiosity, and Beth's growing anxiety could not prevent them hearing what she wanted to keep veiled for now.

'Turn it off, Hazel. We need the truth not sensationalism.'

'We have to know what's going on,' Candace insisted.

At 6 am today a jogger at Pontoon Bay Beach made a gruesome discovery. The mutilated body of what appears to be a young woman, yet to be identified was lying among the sand dunes on the east side of the beach. Anybody with information is asked to contact police immediately. The person or persons responsible are still at large and residents and holiday makers are advised to stay off the beach and the area around the beach until further notice.

VRONEGG WANTED TO THROW UP. Mutilated? How? Who? Why? Eastside of the beach? Her head hurt with the horror of the scene she saw the night before. The drumming of *was it the same three,* left her weak.

'I feel sick. Mum, I need to lie down.' Beth spun around in time to hold her up before she blacked out.

She opened her eyes to Beth and Candace fanning her and swabbing her forehead with a cool cloth. Hazel stood by with a glass of water, anxious and worried. She had never witnessed someone faint before.

'How are you doing Neggie?' Beth uttered one forbidden, endearing version of Vronegg's name in her concern for her daughter.

'I'm okay, I need to go upstairs.'

All three assisted her upstairs and gave her some quiet space.

'It's that bloody corn I warned her about, it will be another day before her tummy settles.'

'It would be a mix of everything, yeah the corn, and this shocking news that there was a murder happening here while we slept.' Candace offered in Vronegg's defence.

VRONEGG LAY face-down on the bed, trying to shut out everything that had happened since last night. Beth came in and sat on her bed.

'Has that news disturbed you? Candace thinks it might have.'

'Disturbed? Aren't we all? Why would it only affect me? Stop talking about me when I'm not there!'

'Calm down, Roni, we all care about you, that's all.'

'Stop with the silly names mum!'

'Okay, sorry, it will take some time for me to stop my loving derivatives of your name. I will let you sleep and will check in on you in an hour.'

She turned away and faced the wall.

Beth understood Vronegg's sensitivity to the pain of others. She recalled Vronegg's week of tears when their neighbor's fox-terrier was killed by a careless driver. A mild sedative calmed her then.

Hazel and Candace watched a movie after breakfast. Police

cordoned off the beach from the end of the cul-de-sac all the way down to the east side where the body was found.

OFFICER VENTER POPPED over on his door-knocking rounds in the neighborhood for any information that would lead the police to the perpetrators of this heinous crime.

'Hello officer. There are four of us in the house, three teenage girls and me.'

'Thank you, mam. Do you mind if I speak with each girl? You may be present during my questioning.'

'Sure, except that my daughter has been unwell since yesterday and might not be up to talking.'

'That's fine, I'll talk to you and the two girls. You can pose the same questions to your daughter and report to me if there is anything you think I should know.'

Vronegg stood at the top of the stairs, out of view, relieved that the officer would not question her about the events that unfolded overnight.

One by one they answered all questions asked. Vronegg caught what the officer said to her mother before he left.

'We have to get this person who did this. The body is unidentifiable — who would do something like this? Only a beast or the devil I tell you. Please keep the young ladies indoors until further advice.'

'That will be a tad difficult but now they know the seriousness of the matter they will comply. It might be better if we headed back home if they must be confined indoors. We come out once a year for the sun and the sea and some relaxation.'

'It's up to you if you want to leave the area but let me know if you are doing so. Please be cautious. This is the worst case I've had to work on in my entire career. These parts have always been peaceful and welcoming, and now this.' The murder rattled officer Venter, the inhumanity he would have witnessed in varying degrees was never this gruesome. It left him saddened and agitated.

Vronegg had a sudden change of heart and came down as fast as she could.

'I can answer your questions officer I feel a little better now.'

'Are you sure, miss?'

'Yeah, let her do it, officer.' Beth added.

'I'll be brief. What time did you go to bed last night?'

'Around nine o'clock.'

'Did you hear any unusual sounds earlier and later in the night if you were awake. Your mum says you had a restless night.'

'I came down for a drink of water. I don't know what time it was. Everyone was asleep. The house was still. I heard nothing except music wafting over from the neighbor's house, I think.'

'Did you look out the window at any point or did you step out onto the balcony?'

'No, I don't go out onto the balcony at night and I did not look out the window. I went back to bed.'

'Thank you for that. If there is anything, no matter how minor you think it to be, tell your mum to call me. Get well soon, miss.'

'Thank you, officer.'

She felt ashamed for lying. The officer was a considerate man, yet she could not bring herself to say what she saw. She had no distinct vision. All she saw were three figures in what appeared to be an argument. This scared her, it could be the motive for the murder. Now she had to protect herself from going mad with the collision of guilt, truth and fear that left her more exhausted than the disruption her upset tummy caused.

Early the next morning Beth left Pontoon Bay Beach with three angry teenagers.

Candace and Hazel glum-faced, for no sensible reason blamed Vronegg for their early departure.

Nobody was apprehended for the crime — this left Beth no option but to go home as Jemima requested.

News broadcasts reported fleeting bits of information as the year progressed, pointing to a cold case.

THIS YEAR BETH had her way again, and all four set out to Pontoon Bay Beach. Jemima was arriving the next morning.

Candace and Hazel were chirpy as usual and Vronegg silent.

A year later nothing had changed.

'This might be our last trip together. I'm heading off to Uni next year and who knows where we will all be in our lives from this point on! Come on, smile Vronegg!' Candace laughed.

'It will be a sad day for your mother and I when you all go off into your adult lives,' Beth moaned. 'I hope we can still come out on holiday sometimes.'

'I may be the only one still with you and mum,' Hazel said with down curled lips.

'We will hang onto you for as long as we can. These older girls will miss out on the fun we'll have!' Beth laughed. She loved their yearly trips to Pontoon Bay Beach.

Amidst the chatter, all Vronegg could think of was the scene on the beach. She stopped paying attention to the news around the murder and nobody spoke of it again.

Beth looked at her in the rear-view mirror. She knew her daughter was uncomfortable with returning to the place that had disturbed her the year before, in more ways than just being unwell.

'Once that sea-air hits you, you will feel much better.'

As much as Vronegg loved the beach, she hated being pounced on and thrown into the water. A near drowning incident at a children's party many years earlier wired her fear. Guilt for not being close to her baby girl made Beth an over-protective mother — the bane of her Neggi's life.

As they turned into the cul-de-sac, they were unprepared for the carnival sight that met their eyes. The usual stillness on the street now teemed with glistening bodies, multi-colored vans housed their wares for sale and reggae music blared across the beach way. The only fixed stand was a sprawling corn shop — a scar on the street — large and looming with a huge corn cob dangling off the roof.

'Wow, what's happened while we were away? I wonder if this goes on every day.' Candace said.

'I hope not!' Vronegg said for the first time since they left home.

'The sign of changing times!' Beth laughed. 'Did you see that corn stand, Vronegg? We can check it out once we get settled. They would have good refrigeration and run a hygienic operation, I'm sure of that.'

People milled around, carefree. licking ice-creams and sipping large sodas.

Hotdogs, beachwear, rustic costume jewellery, sunglasses, barbecued corn, chilled fruit and yoghurt were all on offer. The once pristine, peaceful Pontcon Bay Beach was a busy holiday hive with pop-up stores as far as the eye could see. Too many people, is all Vronegg thought.

THEY UNPACKED. Beth brought in the mail jutting out the letter box at the front of the house. Her heart did a dive when she read the flyer.

Welcome holidaymakers and returning residents.

Forewarned is forearmed is our motto here at Pontoon Bay Beach. You must remain vigilant, when you are on the beach this season. The investigating team have not resolved the tragedy of last year and the perpetrators are still out and about somewhere. Execute care and call police anytime you feel unsafe or suspicious about anything or anyone.

Keep safe. Happy holidays!

– Police Department Pontoon Bay Beach Station.

Beth dreaded reading the newsletter to the girls.

Candace and Hazel took no notice, but Vronegg grabbed it from Beth and ripped it up.

'It's just the police being cautious after sleeping on the job last year. That poor girl could be alive today if they had had night-time beach patrols!'

Vronegg's outburst was unexpected.

Guilt for withholding information is a poison that freezes for a brief time, but melts when triggers add heat to an unsettling memory. A shocked Beth suggested they head to the beach to calm down and enjoy what they had left of the day. She suggested that barbecued corn was her first treat for the holiday season.

'It's a big stand so there could be some interesting flavours!'

Vronegg followed her mother down the street to the corn stand.

As Beth predicted, it was a corn-lovers haven, chilli-corn, honeyed-corn, paprika-corn, sweet-and-sour corn, caramel-corn, chocolate and strawberry flavoured corn! Three people were in attendance, a middle-aged man and his wife and a young man that Vronegg recognized as the same person, the make-shift vendor who had turned up on the beach last year. He smiled remembering seeing her before but said nothing. She looked away.

They sat at the beach munching and licking up butter, honey and spice off their hands when Vronegg said she knew the young man at the corn stand.

'Why didn't you talk to him?' Beth asked in surprise.

'He's seemed the silent type, all he said was, *hello* and *thank you.*'

'Hmm...' is all Beth murmured. She dared not say he was a kindred spirit for fear she would ruffle Vronegg's already unsettled mood.

Hazel called her mother to let her know that corn heaven awaited her arrival the next day. Jemima too, loved barbecued corn. She loved her corn grilled to the fullest, almost black on one side and a rich golden brown on the top and bottom ends. Beth said she would have a chat with the owners of the corn-shop about whether they were a permanent fixture on the beach now.

They retired early that night, exhausted from the drive, sun, saltwater, and indulgent corn tasting.

A thumping sound on the front door woke them around 7 am. Officer Venter stood at the door with his unchanged serious disposition.

'Officer Venter this is a pleasant surprise. How are you?' Beth crooned, always bright that early in the morning.

'Sorry for my early visit, but I believe the sooner the better.'

Beth caught her breath, déjà vu — her mind reeled to 1978 — was there another murder?

'This time there is a sex-pest on the beach, late in the after-noons, harassing young women. I remembered you visited with your girls and thought it best to forewarn you. We've had at least a dozen complaints in the last two days.'

'My goodness, we just got here and did not expect to hear this, thank you, for the heads up. I will warn the girls. They don't go out on the beach alone now, after last year.'

Vronegg was unhappy, 'Why do we keep coming here if the place is no longer safe. You should sell this house.'

'Calm down, we don't have to make drastic changes, just listen to the advice from the police. This place is teeming with holidaymakers so it can't be all bad, right?'

'Be cautious while on holiday, what a joke! I should have stayed with grandma.'

Candace and Hazel were silent, they had never heard Vronegg explode this way with her mother. Candace broke the ice by saying they were lucky to have officer Venter keeping them informed and they should look out for each other with extra care.

A quiet day passed with swimming, but Beth prohibited

hikes into the sand dunes, and they needed to be nearby as Jemima was due to arrive that day. After a barbecue lunch Candace asked if anyone saw the social media posts of the man harassing young women on the beach. Beth turned on the television. An identikit image of the offender made Vronegg gasp.

'What's wrong? Do you know this face?' Beth asked in a hushed tone.

'Oh my god... I don't believe it... it's the face of the boy who was with the corn vendor's son last year. They ran the makeshift stand. He said nothing, never looking up, never greeting nor smiling.'

'We have to call the officer, right away. Are you sure about this?'

'Well, as much as I remember, he is.'

Officer Venter listened to everything Vronegg described and asked Beth if she would allow her to identify the person in a line up. Vronegg agreed and Beth went with her once they had found him and brought him in. The identikit alone was not enough proof that he was the culprit. Later that day, Vronegg stood on the balcony when she saw the police vehicle leave the corn stand. It drove past the beach house with deliberate slowness. A face looked up at her from the back-seat — it was the corn-stand owner's son... staring up at her, no smile, just a cold stare. Her tummy churned, her skin was cold and clammy, she stepped back inside.

First the police questioned the corn-stand owner's son and took him in to the station. He broke down saying that his friend killed the young woman last year because she did not want to date him anymore. He had a violent temper and their frequent arguments forced her to end the relationship. Summer heat, spurned love and jealousy are a lethal combination.

The corn-shop owner's son was involved in the skirmish that night in 1978. He left when he thought the problem was resolved. The young men had not spoken to each other since that night and the corn owner's son remained silent when the young woman was reported missing and later forensic investigation revealed her identity.

Vronegg breathed a sigh of relief once the perpetrator was in custody. She kept away from the corn stand in the firm belief that the owner's son knew the truth of what happened that night and did not report it. This left her with the understanding that truth had a way of returning and she could not hide it from herself. He was as guilty as the person who committed the crime — she saw three figures on the beach that night, she was the fourth as a witness to a crime in the making. She too carried the guilt of silence.

No matter what, she promised herself she would never return to Pontoon Bay Beach, and her mother would have to accept that.

CRADLE PROMISE

Know the pulse of the child in the noise of demands

~~~

The summer in Kenya was at its peak in January 1984.
June to October was the parched season, visitors
thronged in July to see the wildlife migration across
the grassland. The wildebeest migrated and returned to the
Serengeti around October.

The Naraka family were prosperous migrant merchants in
Mombasa. After two decades as Indian expatriates they mingled
with the Kenyan landscape, but inside their home cultural practice took precedence over common thought, often in relation to
their promises made to others for their daughter Kendra.

Kendra was in every way a normal teenager, with a preference and connection to Kenyan culture and language as the
community of her birth. She was passionate in extolling her
African heritage, often to the irritation of both her parents. Miles
of stretching savannah was what she treasured in her oneness
with the land, but upon her sixteenth year her parents subjected

her to home schooling — all contact with her African friends ended. Poetry brought her solace when she composed lines on her angst and hopes, hidden in darkness. The African landscape, now, only a vision from her bedroom window brought little comfort to her agony during those first months away from her closest friends, and the school she loved.

The Narakas sent their son Gaurish off to study in America. Kendra remained cloistered in her bedroom. Their father lived for the day he could tell everyone his son was studying medicine, and as a dutiful son, Gaurish played to his father's expectations. He hated being pressured into a field that held no passion for him. He was creative, he loved painting and sketching — his father called creativity a wastrel's obsession.

'Accomplish something worthy, Gaurish, you are nobody if you are not in medicine.'

Gaurish pointed out that Picasso, Rembrandt and a host of favourite artists had wonderful lives doing what moved them, but his father was relentless. He coerced his son to take up medical studies in New York. The Naraka parents pushed Kendra to engage in domestic tasks, the art of Indian cooking was all that mattered to her mother. Her free spirit was reined and shackled to make room for subservience — her kismet.

It began with a subtle grooming, increasing to forceful expectations that she should grasp the sacred knowledge required to maintain a happy husband.

'But I don't need a husband, so why must I pretend I want a husband at all?'

'Every daughter becomes somebody's wife. The time is right to prepare you for that. It's closer than you expect, look at your ripening body.'

Kendra was a tomboy who chose to scale trees with Gaurish and play football whenever she could.

'We cannot have you kicking your legs up in the dust like a wild fellow, that is why your father says you are like the wildebeest!'

For the first time, she had the impulse to defend her values and hopes for her future.

'Wildebeests are God's creation, so why does Dada mock them?'

'No husband will choose you...' Her mother stopped when her father appeared in the doorway.

'What's with that look, how will the food you cook taste great with a face of an angry wildebeest?' He glanced at his wife and both snorted like two churlish drunks who should be kicked out of the tavern for their abominable behaviour. Kendra bowed with averted eyes, her father expected complete submission to him, no quarrels, no views — no voice that's what he demanded.

After her thirteenth birthday, with the first physical hints of adolescence, they barred her from outdoor activities. She struggled then, until at sixteen schooling ceased. Her socialisation abruptly ended. Naserian and Keruba attempted to visit her but never gained admittance into their home. She yearned for Gaurish to come home for a vacation.

Her parents had promised her at birth, from the cradle, to a family from her father's ancestral village. They had a son two years older than her. Her parents were to hand her over as soon as she turned seventeen to prepare her for her wedding ceremony. Her sixteenth year rolled along this way until Gaurish made his annual visit home.

'Can you please speak to Ma and Dada to send me back to school? I am so lonely, and sad.'

Her pleas agitated him — he had no control over his father's actions. It was much the same for him, he did as he was told. America gave him freedom but in Mombasa he had to play the docile son.

'How do you expect me to do that, without being punished for trying? You know the rules around here, Dada is king. Don't give him ammunition to call you a wildebeest in his derogatory manner, you dislike it from the glowing things you say about the strength and beauty of the animal.'

'Ma won't let Naserian and Keruba into the house to see me, when they come calling. Why are they doing this?'

Gaurish knew the reason but dared not tell her for fear of the outcome from their father. He was counting the days when he could get back to New York. Mombasa was a place he loved but coming home he dreaded. Overcome with pity, he believed his sister needed the truth to help her mentally and emotionally prepare for the future their parents had carved out for her.

'They are preparing you for your marriage to somebody in Dada's village. They will send you there next year to prepare for the nuptials and train to serve your new in laws.'

Kendra understood but did not accept the cultural drill her girl cousins had undergone. Living in Kenya had not altered her parents' ancient practice that made young women objects to be dispensed with as soon as possible after puberty. Disbelief filled her, she looked at her brother with accusation burning in her eyes.

'You're lying, no they won't do this. Dada will want me to study medicine too. I want to be a ladies' doctor. This will make him very proud of me.'

'I had to tell you, because I love you. You need to prepare for this. He will follow through with this cultural rite for girls, remember what happened to Meena?'

'She was miserable and died before her baby was born, I believe she killed herself.'

'Don't say that! You will be in a lot of trouble with Dada if he hears you say that. What we believe does not matter. How can you not understand that by now?'

'So, you just accept it? You are the prince and Dada the king? What do you have to fear? You are a man now, living your big-shot life in America? I want my life too.' She was close to tears but held back, afraid her mother would walk in on them demanding answers to her million questions.

'Don't do this, not now. I must help Dada in the store, that's the reason he flies me home each year. He will be out buying some produce later and I must get in early. We will talk again, soon, I promise.' His heart was breaking seeing his intelligent, beautiful, compassionate sister crushed this way.

'Are you happy, Gaurish? Please be honest, are you?'

He refused to answer her and walked out the room with his hands pressed in his pockets, his shoulders hunched. To protect his sister, he had to be careful with what he said to her. Her emotions were fragile and, she was lonely.

Her mother called out to her, 'Kendra, hurry, stop dilly dally-ing, learn how to cook sweets today. Get into the kitchen, now!' She had hardened in her interactions after Kendra probed for the urgency to have her trained in cooking elaborate meals.

She could not hold back anymore, she wanted answers.

'Ma, I know you are training me for marriage. Who have you chosen for me to marry?'

Her mother, a rotund woman with a large protruding belly, put her hands on her hips, shook her head and scowled until her eyes disappeared behind puffy slits.

'For now, concentrate on making the sweets, it's an art. Thoughts on your future are of no concern to you, and should not distract the learning of this vital skill. How will any man love you if you can't make sweets? The way to a man's heart is through his stomach. And sweet food given will bring you wonderful delights. Look at your father, he cannot wait for his hot meals each evening and loves me more for serving him.'

'It is my life, Ma, I need to know to whom you are selling me! I have never once heard Dada give you his thanks and praise for a well-cooked meal. How is that love?'

Once said, she realized she had sealed a dreadful fate under her mother's tutelage. She was ready to run out the kitchen when her mother barricaded the door, arms on her hips and a scowl that swallowed her beady eyes.

'What cheek is this that I detect in you? You are an extremely selfish girl! For that you will have a life of hell! How dare you question your Dada's love for me!' She gushed in a vernacular tirade on a child's ingratitude, and the curse of having a daughter who would put both her parents in their graves with her disrespect.

Kendra opted for silence from that day on, she moved around the kitchen like a shadow, working with robotic actions in rolling, tossing, dusting, frying, dipping, and on and on she went. Food was hateful in her world. It signaled her imprisonment in a life with a man she was yet to meet and serve.

Her father sat smugly at dinner and looked at her with pride as she served him the array of sweets she had prepared. Her mother smiled with no sign of her earlier outburst at Kendra's questions on marriage.

'Your mother tells me, you are making fine progress in the kitchen, and that you are keen to marry our choice of husband for you. I am thrilled that you have given up all that poetry nonsense to cook better food.' He walked over to the hallway cupboard and pulled out a photograph. 'Here, come have a look at how lucky you are — this is your future husband, promised between our families when you were in the cradle. What a handsome fellow! Look!'

She squirmed and shot a look at her mother, a nodding, smiling body, living to the letter of her father's decree. By now Kendra knew retaliating was useless. Writing poems was her escape in the stillness of dense Mombasa summer nights, pouring her heart out on the page which she stuffed into her mattress to avoid her mother's condemning eyes. Poetry was her claim to freedom, her only claim to self-expression. Kendra looked at the photograph. It was the face of a young man with a healthy crop of shiny jet-black hair, combed back over his head, his hard, staring eyes unsettled her. She looked away, repulsed, the unsmiling face filled her with dread.

She waited for nightfall, when her parents were in bed after a heavy spicy rice meal. Gaurish was close to returning to America — she had to speak to him. He avoided her after his last revelation of their parents' plans for her future. He hated what they subjected her to but was afraid to speak up to defend his sister. Culture could not be questioned. It was prescribed as holy law in their lives.

It was a stifling night, windows were wide open, not a breeze entered to cool the heavy, hot air, trapped inside. Her father's snores, and mother's heavy breathing with sudden eruptions of coughing, confirmed they were sound asleep. She crept into her brother's room. He slept, dead to the world.

'Gaurish, wake up... Gaurish...' She shook his arm with a gentle nudge to avoid him thinking he was being attacked by house thieves. She sat on the side of his bed.

He stirred, rubbed his eyes and looked at her in wide-eyed disbelief.

'What are you doing in my room? This will get you into a lot of trouble!'

'Shhh... quiet, listen to what I have to say. I need your help.'

'I'm leaving on Wednesday and won't be able to help you with whatever it is you want. If you are expecting me to take you with me that is impossible, and you know it.'

'Yes, I know that, but please take this letter to Naserian for me. I am forbidden to see her, please do this for me.' Her voice cracked, this was her last hope, she knew what would happen if her letter to Naserian was found, but the urgency to reach out to her friend consumed her.

'Explain how I am to do this. I can't go to her home with a letter.'

'She will pass by here in the morning on her way to school so you can slip it to her then.'

'You know if I'm seen doing this, people will assume we are having a love affair, I don't want complications, Kendra.'

'Please, this is all I ask of you, before you leave. Please help me.' She shoved the letter under his pillow. Her desperation tugged at him, he reached for her hand.

'What are you planning to do? I need to be aware.'

'Nothing, it's just a letter to tell Naserian that I miss her and Keruba, and to forgive Ma, for not letting them see me.'

'Yeah, right, and I'm supposed to believe that?'

They heard the toilet flush just as Kendra stood up to return to her room.

'Oh my God, that must be Dada!'

She ran over to the cupboard and jumped in behind her brother's clothes.

'Gaurish, you awake?' She heard her father's voice as he approached the bedroom door. 'Who are you talking to, son?'

Kendra held her breath when he entered the room, she prayed Gaurish would not sell her out to him. She peered through the slats of the pinewood cupboard — her father leaned over her brother. What she heard as he playfully tugged at Gaurish's arm filled her with disgust.

'You old rogue! Did you have a girl in here?'

'No! I must have been dreaming. I was being chased by a mob.'

'Nothing wrong with having a girl in your room, you know, a man has to be a man, it will be between you and me. You don't have to lie to me, son. What do you think I do on the nights away on my business trips?' He tapped Gaurish's head with his knuckles. 'Boredom must be eased you know what I mean. Now go back to sleep, we did not have this conversation, you go back to your dream! What's with you Naraka children and your wild imaginations! Dream up new medical research to make a lot of money so I might retire earlier from this hell-hole.' His sickening laugh made Kendra angry. She had the urge to jump out the cupboard and call him a fraud! Her mother, an astute accountant in her day, gave up her job after Gaurish was born, she served her husband's every waking moment, pandering to his needs, and yet when he was out of town, he disrespected the sanctity of their marriage. Her mother was a devoted, foolish woman. The resentment she felt for her mother melted in that instant, and rage burned against her father.

The dank smell of pinewood and clothes made her gag. She stepped out the cupboard after her father left and crawled to lay on the floor, against the wall, close to her brother's bed until she heard her father's grunting snore as he slipped into a deep sleep. Kendra pondered over her father's infidelity, his dislike of Mombasa, something she had never realized until now. This was her home. It was all she knew and loved. Would her mother relegate her to a life such as her own with a husband as her father had proven to be, a deceptive cad! When she heard a regular familiar deep breathing, it signaled safety to return to her room.

She pondered whether Gaurish would take her letter to Naserian and fell into a fretful sleep, worried about the impending marriage her parents had planned.

On Wednesday morning Gaurish left for America.

The letter was gone.

A week passed, and no news arrived from Naserian, until one night she heard a thud on her bedroom window. She went back to sleep, thinking it might be a bird. Then she heard the sound again. She looked out the window and saw nothing. It was another still, hot night. Then, a dazzling beam of light flickered from across the street. She gasped. Someone was watching her! The light flashed again, her eye caught sight of the paper on the ground. She stretched, leaning forward out the window hoping to grab the paper. It was a little out of her reach. With a daredevil decision she jumped out the window, picked it up and crawled back in, grazing her elbows and knees on the rusty window frame.

The note was from Naserian!

My dearest Kendra
   I was so happy to have news from you. Sit tight. Something is being arranged. We must act soon…

She heard her mother's voice, 'Are you awake, Kendra, why is your light on?'

'Sorry to wake you with the light, Ma, I have a sore, dry throat and was about to get a drink of water.' She shoved the note into the hole in her mattress.

'Come with me, I am a little restless too, with your father away. Let me show you how to make a ginger and cardamom chai to ease your sore throat.'

She trembled at this show of sudden care that her mother had neglected ever since they took her out of school. It was short-lived — she spilt some milk on the kitchen counter.

'What is the matter with you, always clumsy! That's why your father calls you a wildebeest.'

Naserian's letter called out to her, she had to get back to it. She pulled it out from the side slit in the mattress when she got back to bed and read it in a rushed frenzy.

Make your way to the market by 9 am on Saturday. I will meet you there.

The note was unsigned, but she knew her friend's handwriting. She had to contain her nervousness and hide her grazed elbows and knees from her parents. Her father would call her a wildebeest if he saw the scars. She tried to fall asleep with no success. This time it was sleeplessness triggered by excitement, anticipation and the nagging doubt whether she could pull this off while her parents stood guard over her, twenty-four-seven.

Time dragged on until a week later when there was a loud incessant knocking at the front door. Her father was away in Nairobi — she was sure he had another family and children there after she overheard him whispering about his manly pursuits.

Her mother was preparing to leave for the store to assist with wholesalers coming in that day.

'Who is this knocking like there's a war coming!'

Naserian's younger brother stood at the door, distressed, blubbering.

'Good morning Mrs Naraka. Can Kendra come over to our house? Naserian is not well and won't wake up. My mother asked me to bring Kendra over to talk to her.'

'What's wrong with your sister? What illness does she have?'

'We don't know, she falls into an unconscious state and cannot remember where she is. It worries us.'

'I can't come to see your sister. Mr Naraka is out of town and I'm minding the store. I will let Kendra go with you, for just an hour, understand. Bring her back in an hour, not a minute later.'

Naserian was at the market, waiting for her. They hugged and rushed over to a car parked in readiness to whisk them away. Naserian's older cousin, Keanjaho, was driving them to the airport. Gaurish had booked an air ticket to New York for his sister. Kendra froze when she realized this was her final getaway.

'I have no clothes, nothing...'

'I have a few things in a small carry-on bag to avoid suspicion. Your brother arranged everything. He loves you very much.'

After the first sting of emotions — she sealed herself off from guilt. All she wanted was to be with Gaurish. He did not say much but understood the gravity of the situation his sister faced.

On the way to the airport, a police checkpoint was conducting random car checks for a runaway driver who had hit a pedestrian the night before. Anxiety gripped Kendra, she called upon all the gods and goddesses her mother summoned in her morning prayer offerings, to get her to the airport hassle free.

Keanjaho looked at Kendra through the rear-view mirror. Her eyes were shut and her lips moved in a silent incantation. After a cursory check, the police let them go.

Naserian's and Kendra's farewell was filled with gratitude, sadness and fear. She had an hour before her mother would panic and send out a search party. Thankfully the wholesalers would occupy her that morning, so it would be several hours before she acted on searching for her daughter.

Kendra headed to the boarding gate. Keanjaho ran after her and slipped her a note telling her to read it an hour after take-off. She looked at him, curious about what the note might instruct her to do. This covert escape played out like a movie. The boarding gate staff looked at her with suspicion, she thought, or was it her imagination. Kendra was not yet eighteen, there was a month to go, and so much could happen. She tossed aside negativity to grab this chance at freedom.

Soon she shut her eyes and willed herself to sleep — it was the only way to calm her fear. She must have fallen into a deep sleep — she was warm, and her left arm ached from having leaned on it for too long.

The woman sitting next to her touched her arm, 'You haven't ordered your meal, the air-hostess said she will be back to take your request.'

'Thank you. Is it morning or night? I must have slept for a long time.'

'It's morning, dear,' the kind woman said.

The smiling face of the air hostess leaned over to her, 'What would like this morning?'

Kendra had no desire to eat anything these days, nervous energy killed her hunger.

'Buttered bread and tea, please.'

'Is that all? How about some cheese and cold meats to go with it?'

'No, thank you, just bread and tea will do.'

She had traveled nowhere on her own before. Her father took control of ordering meals for her mother and her whenever they flew to London to see his sisters, choosing what he liked to eat to finish what they couldn't. This was her first taste of independence. She remembered the note that Keanjaho slipped her. She pulled it out from the side zipper pocket of the bag Naserian had packed.

The faint scrawl, from what might have been a hesitant, hurried hand read:

Kendra, please do not think me rude. Nobody knows, not even Naserian. I was too afraid to tell anyone, and I did not want to disrespect your friendship with my cousin. You both are like sisters. Please know I have been a great admirer for a long time but was afraid to tell you. I don't know if I can ever feel for another this way. I want to come to New York and can be there in six months to tell you, face-to-face. I would like to see you and Gaurish, even if you do not feel for me as I do for you.

Until then… I will be in touch. Keanjaho

Kendra had long admired Keanjaho but saw him as someone she idolized as the perfect guy. Not for a minute had she imagined that he felt the same way. Her heart skipped several beats, a hot flash passed through her, and her eyes filled with tears. So near, yet so far in the restrictions her parents imposed on her. She could have known love sooner, had joy… She stopped herself, knowing that would never have happened with her parents' constant surveillance, to fulfil the cradle promise they made for her future.

Gaurish met her at the airport, his face etched with concern. He ran up to her, scooped her up into his arms as he did when she was a little girl.

'I am so glad you made it! We are not out of danger yet, keep indoors until your eighteenth birthday. This will be difficult as you have had to do this at home, well it's not home anymore, is it? I'm applying for guardianship over you, and with good fortune we can have a better life.'

'What if Ma and Dada call you to tell you I'm missing?'

'I'll say I don't know what has happened to you and will only reveal the truth once you are safe to remain here.'

'I'm worried, for you. Dada will cut the funds to you once he knows you took me out of Kenya.'

'I've worked things out, don't worry that troubled head of yours. I will tell you more when we get home, once you've rested.'

'What if the authorities make me go back, it will be worse, you know?'

'You are not going back, trust me. I've arranged a private tutor to help you prepare for your university entrance requirements, if that is what you want. You don't have to do anything you don't want to do.'

Kendra stared at her world-wise brother. He had it all mapped out. He was giving her the opportunity of a lifetime, and she had to make the most of the sacrifice he made for her. She decided not to tell him about Keanjaho's letter just yet.

Two days later their parents called Gaurish, raising their concern that Kendra had not returned from Naserian's home since Saturday.

'Have you spoken to Naserian's parents?'

'I'm not stupid son! Don't you think that is the first thing I did!' Mr Naraka bellowed down the phone.

He plonked the telephone down on Gaurish when he suggested that Kendra must be safe if they had not found her body.

Gaurish told his sister he had moved out of the university digs and they were moving into an apartment in Manhattan. He gave up his medical studies and took a job with a large company that would fund any studies he wanted to pursue. They needed the money to survive because within days of Kendra's departure, their father cut off Gaurish's funding. A son that disrespected him and possibly fooled him was disowned in a blink.

Kendra worked hard, applied for a medical seat at the university and joined a poetry club. She was growing whole again, although every time she saw a little girl being chastised by her mother, she feared for the child. Gaurish said that family name and honor meant more to their parents than their children's happiness and safety.

They could never go back to Kenya, the land they knew and loved as home.

A year later in the heat of another American summer, Keanjaho arrived in New York. Her heart surged as she walked up to him and melted in his embrace. She knew he was to be a significant part of her future. Gaurish stood in the background holding his partner's hand, whispering, 'She's going to be okay. I know it.'

STILLED HEART

Fury and fire cannot still a loving heart

~~~

G unshots rang out in the distance — Hans thumped down on his piano drowning out the reminder that changed his life forever.

He spent hours in the dining room, huddled over his piano writing and playing music that set his heart aflame. The sounds were sonorous, reflecting his pain, a sadness that remained a memory he would not forget — did not want to forget.

His early morning walk, a year ago was no different to any other day. He set out earlier with the warmth of the day rising. A pair of well-worn joggers, and comfortable track pants were a familiar sight as he strode down the street, passing houses sitting in snug stillness. Some residents in this friendly little street raised their hands to acknowledge him in his daily ritual. Wilhelmstadt Strasse was a neighborhood of elderly couples living their empty nest years in quiet solitude. Hans, Ingrid and two-year-old Lara were a welcome addition to this quiet suburban street. Each went about their business with the knowledge that if they needed neighborly help, all they had to do was ask.

Ingrid and Hans married later in life, both well into their forties giving precedence to their academic lives, now they were proud parents to Lara, a child they had not planned nor expected in their busy middle years. Lara's birth altered the pattern of their lives. They both worked part time at the university sharing Lara's care. They met and fell in love when Hans was in his final year of study for a master's in music, and Ingrid was a newly appointed professor of literature. Their secret relationship lasted the year until they parted ways when Hans took up an offer to work with an orchestra in Sweden. Ten years later they met at a university alumni dinner and picked up the relationship. They married six months later with a greater sense of the need to put down roots with the experience they'd gained. This was Hans' final return home. Lara was raised away from the glare of academic life, hence the choice to live in a little town a long way off from the university.

Hans's early morning walk was no different to any other that day, except for the unsettling presence of armored vehicles, vacant front verandahs, and quieter streets. Ingrid was heavy with flu, he left her asleep with Lara when he set out to get some supplies. Ingrid was a slight woman, and with no appetite since the onset of the flu, she was thinner and weak. All the doctor ordered was bed rest and plenty of fluids. He remembered his mother's spicy vegetable soup, as a child, to fight off flu and colds and decided to try his hand at cooking. He had to get back to work, the next day, with semester exams coming up and students needing extra preparatory sessions.

As he approached the town centre, an eerie feeling fell over him when he saw posters of smiling fresh faced soldiers looking down at him, chilling him on this somewhat warm morning. When the posters went up was a mystery, he had walked that way the day before when the streets were bustling.

He stopped for bread and eggs. The jolly red-faced store owner greeted him with his usual spontaneity.

'Hans, good to see you, my man! Right on time, fresh bread is just out the oven. How's Ingrid and Lara? When am I going to see their beautiful faces again? It's been a while.'

'Morning Gunther. I would love some of that freshly baked bread. It'll be good with the soup I'm making for Ingrid. She has the flu, a bad strain, Lara is well, thank you. I'll bring them over soon, perhaps on Sunday if Ingrid is feeling better then.'

Gunther's spontaneity clouded in a deep frown, he grabbed Hans's hand and pulled him to the back of the store.

'I'm not happy with these prowling vehicles, posters, and damn soldiers parading around. Customers are afraid and foot traffic has slowed down today.'

'Ja, it's not good, it feels different this morning with those vehicles around, but we must keep our chins up and go about our lives as usual, Gunther.'

'Ja, ja, you're right, Hans.'

Hans's optimism belied his impending gloom and irritation with the recent change to his peaceful town. It had been building up in the past six months. He joined the resistance movement for solidarity against violence, to voice his frustration on the tacking down of social freedom. Ingrid was unaware that he had joined the movement or that he attended resistance meetings on Wednesday nights. She believed he was hosting additional classes for struggling students. As much as she supported his anti-violence sentiments, she insisted that they had to keep a low profile. Family was everything to her. His first allegiance was to family, protecting his family from the brewing threat of instability was necessary. Both their parents had passed on, leaving Lara with no grandparents on both sides. Ingrid's home was an orphanage. She had no knowledge of her family history.

The resistance movement prized its ideology on non-violence, any member contravening the values faced immediate expulsion. Hans turned off the television in the house during

Lara's wakeful hours. She was a dreamy child with parents who lived for music and books. Protecting her beautiful spirit was paramount. Ingrid was a realist and proclaimed that protecting Lara from the horrors of violence and inhumanity would be detrimental to her perceptions of the world, and could mar her judgement in later years.

'She needs to know about the shortcomings of the world, Hans. These are growing more intense and diverse every day.'

Their arguments were short-lived with Hans holding onto, 'We should preserve her innocence for as long as possible, the essence of her being will flourish and when the time is right, she will decide how she sees the world, let's not plant seeds to make her fearful now.'

Literature gave Ingrid her lens on life, and Hans immersed his reference to the world through music. In recent weeks, his music took on a haunting sadness with the coming of chaos written in the sky.

AFTER SHOPPING at Gunther's store, Hans walked to the green-grocer for herbs and vegetables for the soup he was to cook. Mrs Bauer's store was empty, not abuzz as it was, at this time in the morning. She shuffled up to him with swollen ankles. Well into her seventies, she was determined to keep working, running the store on her own. The freshness of nature was her explanation for why she was alive to continue doing what she loved — providing healthy, fresh food for locals. She peered at Hans from above her spectacles, or her eyes were lost in a misty fog behind the thick lens.

'Ah, good to see you, as always, Hans. How are your lovely girls?'

'Good to see you too, Mrs Bauer, Lara is well, Ingrid has the flu. I need some vegetables for a robust soup.'

'Ja, it's soup she needs, you are a good husband Hans. A great one, I should say.' She nodded and smiled at him.

'Oh, you flatter me too much! Be careful now, I might move in with you instead!' he laughed and had Mrs Bauer chuckling.

'Always making jokes! Can I suggest you add a little ground beef in that soup? Beef will give Ingrid strength to fight the flu. It's a terrible strain this year they say.'

The town was a large family, each knowing the other, each caring for the other.

In the background discontent grew.

Hans thanked Mrs Bauer and crossed the street to get to the butcher for some meat as she suggested. Halfway across the street he heard an urgent, deafening, wailing siren followed by the hurried pulling down of shutters, and then silence when the siren stopped in mid wail. He spun on his heels and saw Gunther waving frantically from behind half drawn shutters for him to hurry over. Hans shook his head and sprinted back towards Wilhelmstadt Strasse. The silent, deserted street erupted with soldiers heavy rhythmic stomping. They yelled out to Hans — he was the only civilian on the street.

'Get inside, now, get inside, off the streets, now!'

The siren wailed again in one, long, unending howl.

The muscles in Hans' thighs and calves burned, he tried to take deep breaths to calm the foreboding rising within — he had to get home. The faster he ran, the hotter he felt and the slower he moved... anxiety sucked the air from his lungs. Then almost out of nowhere, there appeared in the sky, an advancing black spot, like a gigantic swarm of bees, then it appeared to be blackbirds, he squinted up into the sunlight elevating his pace with thoughts fixed on Ingrid and Lara. He had to get back to them! The black swarm came closer buzzing... a loud explosive sound and a gigantic ball of orange fire is the last thing he saw.

'Sir, sir, wake up!'

Hans looked up at the anxious face of a young nurse.

'Sir, we need the bed, many patients are waiting for a bed. Please, you must try to sit up, here lean on my shoulders.' She inclined towards him, lowering herself almost to a kneeling position.

Hans was ready to jump out the bed, he tried and slumped over — he tried again and slumped over.

The wide-eyed nurse looked at him, unable to conceal her emotions, ready to burst into tears.

'Wait sir,' she pulled a wheelchair close to the bed, 'lean on my shoulders, please, and swing yourself into the seat.'

Under the covers all he saw was blood stained sheets below his bandaged thighs. He had the urge to stand up, he felt his toes tingle.

'My legs… my legs… what happened…'

'You got caught in the air raid, sir, both your legs… we could not save… I am so sorry, sir…'

'How long have I been here?'

'A while sir.'

'How long, nurse?'

'Two weeks, you stirred for the first time, last night, shouting out two names, Ingrid and Lara. Are they your daughters?'

Horror surged through his veins, he choked in a coughing fit.

'Two weeks! My wife Ingrid, and my daughter Lara, where are they?' His voice rose then faded…

He grabbed the nurse's arm, shaking his head, his eyes haggard with disbelief.

'I don't know sir, I'm sorry…'

'Why are you sorry, where are they?'

'I'll wheel you to the office down the corridor, they have the survivors' list there, you can check through for the whereabouts of your wife and daughter.'

The word 'survivor' made him dizzy. Where were his beloved girls? Were they not asleep at home as he had left them?

The stony-faced man at the office with the dreaded survivors' list said, 'I'm sorry their names are not on the list.'

'That's not possible, where could they be?'

'Which street do you live on?'

'Wilhelmstadt Strasse.'

The man looked at him, frowning, 'I'm afraid not many houses survived the blast on that street.'

Hans put both hands over his ears — he did not want to hear what his heart dreaded and his mind knew.

'I need to check for myself, I have to go to the house now!'

'Rubble is being cleared out from the entrance. It will only be safe to check in about two days.'

'Two days? Safe? What is safe anymore?'

HANS REFUSED TO SLEEP, nor eat. He sat in the wheelchair for two nights until he was taken down to Wilhemstadt Strasse by car.

He peered out the window as the car crawled into the dusty, rubble strewn entrance of the street. Two houses to the right, and three to the left lay in a collapsed mess, at the far corner of the street, his house, the only one, stood intact, as he had left it. The houses around his were flattened to the ground or had blown off roof tops and smashed windows. No friendly hands waved a greeting that morning.

A silent young man wheeled him into the house and stood outside.

He moved into the bedroom, expecting... hoping... to see his family, he called out, 'Ingrid, Lara, you okay?'

Not a sound.

The bedcovers sat neatly folded at the foot of the bed. Somebody had put away the unwashed dishes he left in the sink.

Silence.

He called out a few more times with gradual realization that it was pointless.

He refused to leave, he shut the door and slept in the spare bedroom.

AUTUMN CAME AND LEFT, and a bitter winter arrived. War raged in the background of his sorrow. Music filled his days with the pain of long dirges. His finances depleted and his bodily pains increased with no money for medication. In desperation he placed an advertisement for a lodger. Medical bills mounted, and the house was falling to wrack and ruin. Ingrid would be back and unhappy that he neglected to keep the house tidy as she had left it. He hoped he could get help before she returned to assist him upkeep the house.

He stared out the window at snow piling layer upon layer in cold whiteness. He heard a faint knock on the door and reached to turn on the lights and stopped. With unpaid bills, there was no electricity in recent weeks. He lit the gas lamp on the dining room table and wheeled himself to the front door.

In the dimness of the entrance he saw the faint outline of a man who told him he had come to see the room advertised.

In the gas-lit room, the young man appeared to be in his late twenties, lean and clean shaven. He said he worked at the hospital.

Hans told the prospective lodger he had a basement room to let. He left Ingrid's and his bedroom untouched — it was his mausoleum to his wife and daughter.

The young man looked around the basement. He had not expected such a big space and accepted the offer. He explained that he was in the middle of writing his memoir and needed a quiet place.

He agreed to cook their meals some nights and maintain the yard for a reduced rental rate.

Hans's pain eased with the medication he could afford and there was enough soup for two every night of the week.

And so, the winter passed with the young man's respect for Hans's privacy. Each asked no questions of the other, living under one roof in their separate worlds.

One humid summer evening, Hans wheeled himself out onto the verandah.

His lodger heard his movements and stepped outside.

'May I join you?' he asked.

'Ja, you may. I will go in soon.'

'I have completed my memoir and wondered whether you would like to be my first reader. I am keen for your thoughts.'

'Congratulations! That's quite an achievement! Do you trust me to read your memoir?'

'Thank you, Hans. There is no reason not to trust you, you have been very kind to me. I will leave the manuscript on your piano in the morning on my way to work. There is no pressure for you to rush into reading it. Take your time.'

They wished each other a pleasant good night and Hans sat outside for another hour, lost in dreams and hopes that by some miracle he would see Ingrid approaching the house with Lara beside her. He recalled with tenderness the days when he took care of Lara while Ingrid was at work. She would listen to him playing the piano, and clap when he finished a piece. Ingrid taught her to show appreciation for her father's music. He longed to see them both or to know what had happened to them. Not knowing, left him with no closure, it was his living death.

The next morning, he picked up the young man's memoir, poured a cup of coffee and read.

I was born with the promise of a bright future in a beautiful land. You only know pain when that promise is stolen. There is no certainty, and expecting it leads to misery. War is the selfish act that claimed my parents and beautiful sister. I was safe at work when the orange ball fell out the sky altering my life forever. I wait for my end, when will it come? I cannot choose the time. All I can do is help save another life that has gone through my fate.

Hans put down the manuscript, it was as close as reading his own memoir. He could not go on reading.

He spent the rest of the morning mulling over the words, *all I can do is help save another life …*

The letter the university had sent him almost a year ago sat unopened on the hallway table. Now he felt compelled to read it.

Dear Hans Schmidt,

We would like to offer you assisted return to work conditions as your skills are much needed in our music department. We will provide transportation and anything else you might need to continue working with us.

Hans looked down at his legs and smoothed his hand over a photograph of Ingrid and Lara. He heard Ingrid's voice whisper, 'Do it Hans, please do it.'

He called the university and signed the dotted line to begin work in the spring.

At his first lecture, he introduced himself.

'I am Hans Schmidt, husband of Ingrid and father of Lara. I am a musician and teacher and I'm here to help you through my story. Take every minute you can to create something to reach others. A stilled heart deepens sadness.'

ADRIFT

The beauty of a soul is a hidden gem

~~~

I t's the eve of my wedding, I should be happy, but an overwhelming sadness washes over me.

Sleepless nights are back, I cry and sob in my sleep, and Jordan has been patient with me. But, how long will he be able to sustain this? I am needy in a range of ways. I will let you decide if this is indulgent on my part or warranted. I don't have an opinion on that when my mind is in turmoil. I don't really have family here in America and have no one who can step into my shoes to see my world through my eyes. All the love in the world from a devoted partner and all the education you pursue cannot erase the angst of the soul.

My fear tonight is that I will meet many of Jordan's extended family members for the first time and I know my past will create curiosity. Jordan knows my history and has tried to help me accept that it is nobody's business but my own. I prepared a speech on who I am and how we met — now I'm petrified of judgement. Jordan says what others think does not matter — how do I convince myself...

Dare I reveal my secret... do I dare?

I FEEL MYSELF SLIPPING BACK... nausea rises, wind cuts through my skin, sun scorches my head. How do I convince my sixteen-year-old self that now at thirty-nine I deserve to be happy? Where do I begin? Will it ever stop? Just a civil ceremony down-town on our own would have been enough. A huge wedding, a massive banquet makes me ill. I know I agreed for Jordan's sake, but for months I've been uneasy about this day. He says I work so hard and deserve to celebrate our union in style. I like things simple, quiet, no pomp, it's the way I know.

Memory has been my eternal hell and countless therapy sessions have not erased the trauma crawling under my skin. Every time there's the possibility or anticipation I might have to share my life with strangers, the dread and tension surfaces... I shied away from writing down my struggles even though my therapist suggested it. Writing it all is a way of bringing me back into my conscious space — painful memories chastised me with every detail, so I might as well write it. Here goes, I will take a risk to gain the happiness Jordan says I deserve.

MY MOTHER'S stall at the market attracted droves of tourists, not only for the wares they purchased but because her warm joy made everyone who entered the little stall feel special enough to return each time they traveled through. She had beautiful black flowing hair cascading down her back. She pinned her hair in a loose French roll when she was at the market, rushing around, unpacking new supplies and repricing old goods to attract the latest arrival of tourists. My sister was a late child to my parents, born during the war. They took my father in the last weeks before the war ended. We never saw him again. I helped my mother as much as I could with my baby sister, taking on the role of a mother when she was busy.

Our little lives did not last as I thought it would. Rebels confiscated my mother's stall, and our family home in the aftermath of war. A free-for-all attitude permeated the minds of those who felt cheated by the war. Everybody was, but some felt harder done by than others. We were homeless and had to live in a post-war camp set up on the outskirts of the city. Many mushroomed in the days after the bloodbath. My ailing grandmother needed care. My mother's full attention went to her.

One day my mother sat my sister and I down, by this time my sister was three years old. The preposition my mother wanted me to accept is so vivid to this day and fills me with regret for what it offered. The course of my life changed irretrievably after that day. She had mulled over what she wanted for us and was not prepared to accept a refusal.

'Mai, you and your sister cannot continue to live like this. Poverty and disease will kill us all. And you both need to have a decent education. That has been your father's and my hopes and dreams for you.'

'What are you saying, mẹ?'

'I want you to take your sister and go to America to my friend. She is expecting you, it's the only way.'

'What about you, why are you not coming with us? And bàngoại? And bố? How will he know where we are when he returns? No mẹ, please don't make me do this without you.' I cried in fear for what the future might hold for our family.

'I can't my love, bàngoai is too ill to make the trip, and we do not know when your father will return. I will ensure he knows where we are, should he return. You must go, I will follow as soon as your grandmother is well again.'

Jocelyn Narrelli, my mother's friend would take care of us until my mother arrived in America. That was my mother's promise. A man arrived in the middle of the night to transport us to America, I did not understand how this was to happen but trusted that my mother knew best. She was a protective mother, necessity made it essential that we separate this way. For a while.

My mother explained that the man taking us across the sea only allowed two small bags even though it would be a long journey. Her last words are whispers I hear in my dreams and silent waking hours.

'Promise me you will take care of Chau and yourself and not be any trouble to Aunt Jocelyn, until I get to you.' The finality, of those words, meant nothing then. She gave my sister and I an opportunity of a life outside the struggle we would endure if we stayed. The adult me realized that she put her life savings, all her earnings from her little market business, to give us the life she wanted us to have, a life of happiness, love, freedom and the chance to make something of our lives.

A scrawny, tanned man arrived in a small van to take us to the promised land of my mother's dreams. His darting black eyes, and red stained teeth flashed a quick smile that conveyed his agitation. He wanted us to hurry, to rush off, to stop the hugs and endless kisses. He muttered as he picked up our tiny bags, 'too much, too much.'

I turned around, looked at my mother with tears scalding my cheeks, my mother waved running towards the van as if she had changed her mind about letting us go, and then she walked backwards, one slow step at a time, afraid to take her eyes off the van until it disappeared from view.

I never saw my mother again.

The man took us to a camp hidden amongst tall conifers in a dense forest. He instructed us to remain in the tent. I heard voices, children's voices and women's voices and a few men speaking in lowered tones.

The next evening, we walked down to a ravine, clutching our bags. A large wooden boat, more like a bowl-shaped raft waited for us, barely visible in the faint glint of the moon shining a sliver of light onto the water. Scores of people huddled in silence as they jumped onto the boat. Some women needed help. I looked back afraid to jump in when I felt a gentle hand on my head. I whispered, 'mẹ?' The voice of an old woman said, 'Don't look, don't long, move on, or it will make you sad. We must hurry.' She nudged me forward. I jumped onto the boat careful that Chau was safely in my arms. People crouched to offer us a safe landing on the boat. The man threw our bags in behind us. Bodies pressed against each other, foul breath and body odor hung in the air. We were strangers thrown together by war in a quest for a better life. Old, young, newborn and maimed leaned against each other. No face was discernible as the moon disappeared behind a dark cloud. There were deep sighs, I heard a woman sob and a baby cry.

Soon like a giant waking after centuries of sleep, the boat crept forward, rocking a little and then a sweet melodious singing wafted over from the other side of the boat.

'Shhhh, no singing until we hit the high seas, we must be quiet,' the scrawny man hissed.

Chau and I fell asleep.

I dreamt of the day my sister was born. We were at the market when my mother went into labour. I ran all the way back to the house to get my grandmother. I was her assistant, boiling water and running back to the house for more towels. Then I saw the top of Chau's head emerge, a rush of black hair. My heart skipped a beat. Then her swollen closed eyes appeared, she was just beautiful, my precious newborn sister had a fine pair of lungs. My mother, grandmother and I laughed and cried. My mother whispered her name, 'Chau,' which means like a pearl. And so she was with her shiny pale skin, lighter than mine. I held Chau close. I promised my mother I would take care of her, now Chau was my child, a protective instinct took hold. I kissed the top of her head and prayed for our safety and that of the people on board this flimsy vessel, a mere dot on a vast ocean. Thoughts of my father returned, was he alive, was he safe? They took him a week before Chau was born.

Warm sun kissed my arms, and I tried to stretch. With bodies wedged against each other it was impossible to move a limb. My legs were numb, I wanted to stand up. My neck was stiff, and I felt Chau wriggling. I opened my eyes to hundreds of eyes looking at me, no emotions, blank stares. I closed my eyes again thinking, I must be in a dream, willing the scene to go away. I opened my eyes again to my sad reality. We were somewhere on the southern China sea.

I heard the voice that told me not to look back, not too long, don't be sad, and looked into the eyes and kind face of a woman old enough to be my grandmother. She smiled at me. She asked if I could pass Chau across to her. I froze. She was a stranger. I could not hand over my little sister to her. There was no one with her that might be her family. She pushed herself forward trying to reach out for Chau. It was impossible with the multitude of bodies packed in like sardines. A child cried somewhere from the dense middle of the boat. Chau stirred and craned her neck to see who it was. My throat was dry, crusts of saliva around my mouth made me uncomfortable.

I will never forget what happened next, a little boy wriggled until he freed himself to stand up, he must have been about six or seven years old. The boat dipped, people gasped as they clung to the edge and each other, the boy flew off the boat at a projectile angle into the ocean. People shouted out and tried to free themselves to save him. It was impossible. The child disappeared, sinking into the ocean. I clung to Chau, shivering and weeping.

A day of mourning followed. Silence except for the gut-wrenching howl of the mother sent currents of fear through my body. Chau cried, she was hot and thirsty. I rocked her until she fell asleep again. My mother's words played in my head, I felt lightheaded, how was I going to protect and care for Chau when I felt sick.

The third night in the boat was cold. The high winds were icy. Male voices wafted over from somewhere in the distance. The women called out in fear.

'Stay down, stay down, pirates are coming, sleep, close your eyes.'

My bladder was bursting, fear tightened my grip on Chau. I wet my pants and tried not to sob for my sorry state. The voices grew louder as they came closer... then horrible laughter and disgusting belching...

I huddled over Chau, covering her, thinking we would be shot. I was not prepared for what followed. Women's voices yelled in pain, protest and heart-stopping cries. It went on for an hour until I felt a hand on my back. Instinct made me press myself down on my sister, she must not be seen. I arched my back to shake off the person, but I was too weak. In that movement I created a tiny gap between Chau and I, she wriggled free and crawled away from me over other bodies crouching low, curled in tight balls to avoid detection. I looked up to see where my sister was, but I was pinned down with the weight on my back — then, then... I saw Chau's white socked feet tumble over the edge of the boat. I yelled out, 'My sister, please get my sister, she fell over, 'get my sister...'

I must have blacked out because I awoke to the sounds of gunshots.

In the frenzy of those last hours on the vessel, I refused to accept that Chau had fallen overboard, I reached out to feel her warm body, but she was gone — floating somewhere in the sea. I felt the cold barrel of a gun against my temples and heard a voice, 'Get out, get out, now!'

Armed militia escorted us to the campsites set up on the beach. We were on American shores. How we got there is beyond me.

Two days later an officer ordered me to go higher up the beach to a makeshift office, someone had come to see me. I was so afraid, my legs turned to jelly, and I fell over.

'Get up, get up! Someone is waiting to see you!' the uniformed man yelled.

My vision was blurry, I blinked when I saw someone

anxiously moving what appeared to be arms. A woman waved and beckoned me towards her, she scooped me into her arms, sobbing, 'Mai, you made it, you made it! Where's your sister? It's me, Aunty Jocelyn.'

My throat locked, and my tears dried. How was I to explain that sweet, innocent Chau escaped the brutality of the pirates, she was pure and free. Aunty Jocelyn understood and rushed me to the car. 'I'm taking you to a doctor first and then we go home, your new home.'

I felt ashamed and sad that I would never be as pure as Chau and my mother would never forgive me for not protecting my baby sister. I was responsible for her death. How would I tell my mother this?

That was my entrance into America and now today I am rigid with fear on the eve of my wedding day.

I went to school, studied for a history and literature degree and taught history at a local college. Through the years I heard that my mother and grandmother had died and that my father never returned, also presumed dead. I planned to go back someday but fear kept me away. Thoughts of that treacherous boat journey scarred me. I often wonder what happened to the wise woman who told me not to look back, not too long, don't be sad. I never got to know her name. Jocelyn whisked me away before anybody changed their minds about letting me go with her. She died when I was in my final year of college. I was alone until I met Jordan. I insulated myself, not forming any close relationships. It was my wedding, and I had no girlfriends to console me, or to giggle with me. My past infected my joy.

Jordan took almost a year before he plucked up the courage to ask me out on a date. We stood on the same station platform, took the same train and got off at the same station for an entire year. It took me another six months before I accepted his coffee date. Trust was my biggest issue, especially if a man showed interest in me. From women, I steered clear for fear of what conversation they might invite me to join. After three months I told Jordan about my life and expected him to stop calling me, to forget about me, but he proposed, and I accepted. It felt right, he never judged, he was a good listener. It goes with the territory — he was a head therapist in the medical centre next door to the college where I worked. He never psychoanalysed me, but suggested someone I should see to help me relinquish blame for my sister's death. He ensured that the therapist he recommended was not from his centre, he understood, and honored my privacy. Until Jordan arrived in my life, I had no psychological intervention for the trauma I endured. It amazed him that I survived my past demons and had not had a mental breakdown. The therapy helped, I was happier, Jordan said I was more sociable and laughed a lot more than when he first met me. People noticed a change in me, but my years of social isolation, in only connecting with my students, kept them cautious in their interactions with me.

All I ever said to my work colleagues was that I was an adopted child and did not know my heritage. I lived that lie to protect myself. I avoided staff dinners, picnic days and had a storehouse of excuses to keep me separate and insulated. The pirate invasion that night on the boat was something I struggled to reveal to my therapist. It was only possible through hypnosis which I resisted at first. After that session it felt like a rebirth — a huge load was lifted. Secrets and shame were there, but a lightness filled my being. As my confidence grew, my students gained, I could share a part of my personal history in my lessons. This brought profound compassion and understanding, and I know somewhere deep down, they would carry that into their future lives. For me it was enough to know that the travesty of history recurring could be averted if I shared the torment and torture of what my family and people had endured. The telling of my story brought healing.

In the flurry of wedding preparations, I could shelve those dark days in the recesses of my mind. Now sitting in front of the mirror, I see my mother and Chau in my own image — the shame and hate and disgust returned — it is a self-loathing that diseased the mind. I will try to get through my speech and avoid conversations — who was I kidding, curiosity would invite more questions, how was I going to pull this off?

The only thing to save Jordan any embarrassment was to tell him we had to call off the wedding at this eleventh hour. He would be hurt, and soon he would get over it and move on with his life. I could move interstate to another school, but I knew I had to stay in America. It was the promised land my mother wanted for me and my darling sister. God rest their souls in eternal peace.

I sent Jordan a text message and although we agreed not to talk to each other, not see each other for twenty-four hours before the wedding. I had to let him know I was cracking.

He returned my call, I apologised for breaking his tradition of no contact and he said, 'Mai, my love, what good is any tradition if you are talking about calling the wedding off?'

'I don't want to embarrass you with my shameful past... I don't...'

'Shameful past? Never! You and your family were victims of a terrible war. You not turning up tomorrow will kill me, Mai. I know you're strong. You are a survivalist — look at what you've achieved in your life? On your own.'

I believed that if I walked away from this marriage, I would never meet another man like Jordan, unselfish, and caring to a fault.

'I wish my father could be at my wedding to deliver a speech on me, and not me talking about myself.'

Jordan was silent not knowing how to give me this one thing I desired.

'I believe it will surprise you how people will respond to you after you deliver your speech, be yourself, say that you are speaking on behalf of your father because you know what he would have said at your wedding. Bring him back in that moment through your recollection.' He paused and added, 'if you feel it does not work out as I say it would, we can move to another country the next day.'

'Leave the country?' Mai laughed.

'Well, it got you to laugh! Do it, tell the world who Mai is. I know she is adorable, funny, loving and a little too serious sometimes, but a wonderful giving woman.'

The next morning it rained like a drought had broken. Sheets of rain and fog drenched the city. How was I to wear this beautiful pearl studded dress with my mother's, father's, grandmother's and sister's names stitched in every hem. The pearls were my Chau, she would have been a bridesmaid standing beside me, I carried her in every pearl, a thousand of them glittering in every conceivable spot.

That afternoon the rain stopped, the sky cleared, the sun shone in its all its glory like it had never rained at all.

I STOOD up to deliver my autobiographical speech. I stood tall and strong and began.

'It takes a special man to look beyond the flaws of a woman. I am Mai, a refugee who arrived on a boat in America, an illegal boat, I was running away from the ravage of war... with my mother's love and blessing...'

MOVING ON

Remember thy ways when the new beckons

~~~

Society had rejected them for their communal habits in their desire to survive close to the earth, pure and intact — away from a mechanistic modern world.

The Ayar family resided for fifty years in a tight-knit rural family compound called Pucara. They were tough and youthful in appearance, even grandfather Sinchi at ninety-two years was nimble in action and looked like a man half his age, still toiling the land and drawing water from the well. Hard work had calloused his hands, but his face and smile were as cheery as a dawn sunrise.

The metropolis around Pucara grew, sprawling across a vast expanse. Greedy real estate agents approached Sinchi and his son Inti to persuade them to sell up the Pucara site for the development of high-rise offices. While buildings mushroomed around them, Sinchi was stoic in refusing offers to sell, he wanted to preserve the culture and lifestyle of his ancestors.

Four generations of the Ayar family remained intact, those that married into the family embraced the culture and lifestyle like a second skin. The council requested changes to sanitation and their water supply, or they would condemn their small holding in the centre of town.

Fresh vegetables, corn, beans and squash grew in abundance on the property. They brought in chickens to provide eggs for the protein needs of the younger generation, who went to school and worked outside Pucara. A cow, faithful Milly, led to subtle changes with grandfather Sinchi and Inti preparing cheese and yoghurt for the children. They led a simple life. Grandmother Curaca, Inti's mother, and Mama Quilla, Anqui's mother spun their own yarn on an ancient spindle to produce cloth. Basic long skirts and shorts and box-necked shirts was all they needed. Nobody complained when the clothes they outgrew went to the next generation. An organic life that many of the rich and famous desired and paid large sums of money to acquire, was the Ayar's everyday life. Wrinkle and disease free, was a bonus to this lifestyle and cultural practice of selflessness, bravery and shunning aggression. They embraced humility and simplicity when their pioneering family settled in the locality a long time ago. Now they lived isolated, behind the walls of Pucara, as an oddity in the modern world.

While the world grew in vanity and vice, the Ayar's remained unsullied by preserving their culture and heritage.

ON THE MORNING of his eighteenth birthday, Anqui approached Mama Quilla with tears in his eyes and brimming trepidation.

'Mama, life has been intolerable at school all these years, but I pleased father and grandfather. Now that I will study at the university, I am requesting to live outside Pucara while I study, and perhaps once I enter the workforce. I cannot hide and skulk around anymore, it's too exhausting to do this.'

'What are you asking me to do, Anqui?'

'I love my family, I am not leaving in any permanent way, just moving on, but I ask to be granted permission to live in town among the city dwellers. I want to be accepted...'

'Moving on?' Mama Quilla's voice took on a shriller tone. 'How will you survive? You have only known this life, our life, our way?'

'I have to try, please Mama. I cannot move ahead with my professional aspirations if I continue living here, without experience of the larger world.'

Mama Quilla sighed, 'You say, 'living here,' as though it has been a terrible life for you. It will devastate your father and grandfather. They have high hopes for you.'

Anqui struggled for many years at school, the bullying was unbearable. School kids teased him for his homemade clothes, told him he reeked of body odor and mocked him for this simple lunch of corn, beans and potatoes. They laughed at his hair and ridiculed his poor taste in shoes. He took it all with no retaliation, retreating to the river after school, tossing stones into the water, watching it ripple on the surface to calm his anger before he returned home. The girls were not as overt as the boys in their criticisms of him. They walked past him, but their stifled giggles cut deeper than the direct jibes from the boys.

One day when he came home with a bleeding lip, he lied to Mama Quilla that he had tripped on a log on the way home. A group of horrible boys accosted him on a side alley after school. The names they called him lived inside him, ulcerating for change. The taunts as they kicked him to the ground and rolled him in the dirt left him writhing in pain. He hobbled to the river, blood trickled down his chin from his bleeding nose, he worried that he would have to explain his plight to his parents and sister. He cleaned up his face and returned home. The little river at the end of their property was his haven. Grandfather Sinchi had paved the space around the river and placed a few handmade seats and carved rocks on the banks.

His sister caught sight of him limping back to the house and ran in to tell their mother. Mama Quilla rushed out.

'What happened to you? Your lip is swollen, did you have an accident? Look at your clothes, Curaca will be upset, the back of your pants is torn. Are you hurt anywhere else?'

With the speed of a Shinkansen train, Anqui said, 'I fell over, I was stupid and ran home and tripped over a log, that's all. I'm okay, Mama.'

His mother disbelieved every word he said. He knew that look on her face and again quickly offered to wash the dishes and sweep the courtyard for a week.

'That won't be necessary,' Mama Quilla reassured him, 'come let's get you cleaned up. Be warned salt will sting the gaping wound on our lip.'

Today she recalled that day and felt a gnawing realization that her son had endured much and was ready to try out the new world, to see if it would accept him, like he was prepared to accept the outside.

The spirit of the Ayar family was gentle, children received life lessons from their elders, without the threat of punishment. They took all decisions at a full sitting of the extended family. The elders convened a meeting in the dining hall where the family took their evening meals together, sharing myths, legends and fables before they departed to bed. The meeting this evening was of an uncharacteristic nature. One of their own wanted to leave the family fold. It had never happened before. One of them needed freedom.

A quiet group settled down to listen to Anqui's angst. News had slipped out to the family that he was unhappy. The usual merriment at such gatherings was absent, a sombre mood fell over them. How could Anqui defect from a world that protected him?

Inti stood at the front of the room with grandfather Sinchi seated beside him with his head lowered.

'Greetings all. Your brother, my son, Anqui, as you have earlier heard is seeking to advance into the contemporary world to be accepted by modern society as he has declared to Mama Quilla. It unsettles him, he wants change. We have assembled here to figure out his sincere intentions firsthand. As the Ayar motto says, honesty, truth and work. Anqui has been honorable in bringing his sincerity to his mother and we sense that planted in his appeal is the desire to achieve inclusion in the big world.'

Awkward shuffling and faint chatter buzzed through the family.

'He has confessed that he has had terrible struggles outside, at school, that he has not expressed until now.'

Brother Kon stood up after raising his hand wishing to have a voice.

'Father may I speak before Anqui, to provide clarity to him and the inexperienced ones tonight.'

'Certainly Kon. Go ahead. We need everyone to offer their thoughts if possible.'

'Our lifestyle preserved us in peace and integrity for decades, behind the gates of Pucara,' Kon began. 'It's a blessing to have our way of life and values. It's an angry, competitive world out there.' He looked around the room. 'Wanton destruction has tainted the human condition in the modern world. Wars of race, gender and religion add to the mountain of greed that has grown with each decade. This is not as the gods intended. We must contemplate this catastrophic existence in how we can improve the lot of our fellow humankind, rather than fall victim to its vices. I ask Anqui now — are you prepared for the skirmish of such a life that exists outside the solace of Pucara?'

All eyes turned to the red-faced Anqui, a handsome lad whose smile faded as the years passed. His heart was heavy in understanding the truth in Kon's words. Inti nodded throughout Kon's speech and grandfather Sinchi beamed with pride in hearing honesty and truth upheld and scanned the faces in the room. The tide of change was now rising within the walls of Pucara.

'Would you like to respond, beloved Anqui,' Inti asked his son.

Anqui rose with stooped shoulders, guilt riddled on his handsome face. In the family's eyes he was a traitor, yet that was not his intention. They had to believe that he would always be an Ayar and Pucara would always be his home. He needed to catch up with the world for progress.

'My beloved family,' he said without looking up. 'Cast not your criticism nor scorn at me. I ask for this release only to come back to share my findings and understanding from an adult perspective as one who has not only worked but also lived in modern society. I have struggled with this for a long time. My wisdom learned from you, my family, tells me to appreciate more of what I have, but I have to experience difference.'

A hush fell over the room. Anqui looked up, afraid that he might have injured the feelings of his loving family.

'I am not walking away with no intention of returning, quite the opposite. I seek your blessing to gain an understanding for why bullying occurs against our children, and why I have no friends outside Pucara.'

Mama Zara spoke, 'This does not augur well. More heartache will come when you force that which is not meant to be. I fear for you our beloved.'

Young Nusta shot her hand up and blurted out, 'Anqui will find love and bring a young lady home to us. We have not had a new lady in our family for a long time. That will help me write more love stories!'

Nusta was a romantic little girl, dreaming about faraway places and knights in shining armor saving damsels in distress. She loved writing stories and entertained the girls and women in Pucara with her wild imagination.

Anqui responded with an even redder face, 'It's not my intention to find love, just yet, I want to immerse myself in study, work, and the lifestyle outside to bring back greater truths. If I find someone who finds me bearable enough to love and marry and join my family here in Pucara, you will be the first to know, Nusta.' Anqui smiled lighting up every face in the room.

Grandfather Sinchi was happy that Anqui was honest that he did not intend to abandon his family or his values. All he wanted was to bring an education about the outside that had moved eons ahead of them while they stood on the same spot, unmovable.

Inti said, 'As long as you remain true to who you are with the values we have instilled, you can avoid slipping into the ill ways of the world. If you forget this, we are not equipped to help you out of this quagmire. Being authentic is important where every-thing is fake, it's becoming the norm these days, that's the way of the world outside, nothing is as it seems.'

'Father, I agree, I will never let that happen. It will make me far more stressed to do that. I am secure in who I am, trust me.'

Inti looked at his son, afraid that he was too self-assured at just eighteen.

'Take it slow and steady, my son.'

Mama Quilla had to support Inti on this view, 'Wrong ways are easy to fall into when you are searching for a sense of belong-ing. Your father has left you with the wisdom of not assuming you can avoid the pitfalls, that you should slow down and ponder a course of action that is aligned with your Ayar beliefs. Shine the light we've given you on others, especially those who struggle.'

Anqui nodded, bowed to Mama Quilla, 'I give you my word, Mama.'

Letting go was not easy for his mother, she had seen him err more than the other younger ones over the years. He was vulner-able in over trusting and giving too much too soon. She had to let go in the faith that the gods would watch and guide him. Their world had much to teach modern civilization and with

Anqui's debut into the world, there was hope that he could renew humanity to be supportive of each other.

Inti perceived that concern was present in their family community and knew he had to settle their doubts.

'Anqui has a good head on his young shoulders, we have to trust his truth as we trust the truth of each other. I believe he will sustain the values of our generations past and present. It is becoming essential that we embrace change, the good aspects of change that will bring further meaning to us. It is no longer possible to live in complete isolation. A bit of seclusion is needed to keep us peaceful. We can exercise our own caution on matters that do not sit well with us.' Everybody listened without objecting.

Nusta blurted out again, 'I can be Anqui's messenger, he can pass on all he has learned outside and I can write it all down and read it during our evening story telling.'

Inti and Mama Quilla accepted that the tide of change had come to Pucara and rather than lose the younger generation, they had to understand why they needed to be part of the modern world.

What fascinated youth about the outside, terrified the elders inside Pucara.

The youngest in the clan ran towards Inti, 'Please tell them all what I want to be when I grow up, tell them, please.'

Inti smiled, 'Our little one wants to be an astronaut when he's ready. He wants to soar high above Pucara, he says, because he cannot see much of the sky with all the high buildings around us, and he wants to touch the heavens and talk to the gods and bring their new messages back home to us.'

There was a burst of laughter at his innocence, yet truth is what their youngest articulated. They needed new messages as much as they needed to see more of the sky.

Mama Quilla hooked her arm in Anqui's and stepped out into the darkness. She looked up at a small piece of sky with a few visible twinkling stars.

'The stars are out to bless you tonight, son. I know you will return richer to us with the connections you will form, and this will allow us to collaborate with the universe for an enhanced version of what it means to be from the Ayar clan and a valuable part of humanity.'

WANDERING THE EARTH

Night, the subduer, finds the vessel to unveil long forgotten truths

~~~

I am thirty-nine years old.

I feel impending dread in knowing I will be forty in six months.

My life has been strange and wonderful. I cannot say for how much longer, I will withstand being witness to the atrocities of the world. It leaves my days in anxious anticipation of what next and how much more…

I have not been at rest for a long time.

I WAS BORN in a village close to the Limpopo River. My country was in the grip of racial strife. Injustice left the poor in greater impoverishment as the divide grew wider between the rich and the poor. My parents left me orphaned after the Soweto Riots in 1976. Both dead, snuffed out with two gunshots in their backs.

What a terrible day in my country's history — dark days grew in intensity. Here I was, eighteen months old and left an orphan. I was the only child to my young parents. History books tell me about the days of apartheid, but all that I know first-hand are the glorious days of Nelson Mandela and the promise he delivered. The Soweto Riots bloodbath left me in the care of my mother's sister, Aunt Zindi, who would not give me up to authorities as a ward of the state. She said it came with a death sentence. As a child of massacred parents, I was lucky to have the compassion of Aunt Zindi in taking me in, when she had six of her own children in need of her constant care.

Aunt Zindi's home was a warm place except for her great-grandfather-in-law, also in her care. He had the most amazing, transparent grey eyes, feline almost, but there was a strange aura that surrounded him. I can't quite put my finger on what it was — he was a silent man. He sat out in the sun on the stoep, staring across the veld as if waiting for someone to arrive. I wondered whether he was perhaps blind, until one day I tested it out. My boyish curiosity led to me doing handstands and cartwheels to get some reaction from him. His eyes followed my antics in an emotionless stare.

One night in my sixteenth year, on the night of my birthday, a strange vision disturbed me. I woke up crying and shouting, 'Go away, go away!'

Aunt Zindi rushed to pacify me before I unsettled the children. It was a strange dream. I remember being woken by a bright light that seemed to be flicked on by an unseen hand. We never used electricity at night to light up the house, we used candles and gas lamps. Electricity was too expensive and a novelty in these rural parts of the country. Aunt Zindi would purchase a pre-paid card that allowed her electricity usage until the card needed a top-up. Well, money was scarce with six children, including me and her great-grandfather-in law. Aunt Zindi's husband had another family to take care of with a younger woman, and so my aunt was really a single parent. Apartheid left a slow burn, the poor had a sense of something more, but not enough to claim any comfort or luxury.

I was afraid to open my eyes to the bright light — then I felt a soft hand caressing the top of my head. My eyes opened and there before me was the face of an old man, his cold grey eyes looked at my face with fascination. I tried to scream, but no sound left my lips. The old man had long white hair that curled down his shoulders and a beard that hung down to his protruding belly. A cool breeze passed over me and then I let out the loudest yell I could summon bringing Aunt Zindi charging into the room.

'What's wrong, Jacob, why are you screaming like this in the middle of the night, you will disturb the children, stop it now,' she whispered, adding, 'did you have a bad dream?'

I tried to tell her what had happened but words to describe it evaded me. Instead, I pointed to the door. She turned looking at the door in confusion.

'Are you telling me you saw a spook? They don't exist, Jacob. We have God in our home, go back to sleep.'

'It was a spook, Aunt Zindi, I saw... I saw a white-haired man...'

'Well, he's not here, you imagined it.'

'He was here now-now.' My heartbeat was fast and hard, it hurt my chest. I thought I was about to die. Aunt Zindi rolled her eyes, shrugged her shoulders, tucked me in, patted my head and said, 'Please sleep, you can tell me about it in the morning, if you still remember your dream.' She left me staring up at the ceiling expecting the apparition to return.

Nobody would believe what I saw. I kept silent about it but that was not the end. It went on for three nights and recurred every year thereafter, always on the night of my birthday. The dream, after the first night, progressed the next night, I was walking through bushland in long grass encircled by tall gum trees. Then I caught sight of two figures, one a boy perhaps around ten or twelve years old, and an older man engaged in an argument. The man was shoving the boy and saying something that I could not quite hear from where I was standing. The man reached in his pocket for something and then repeatedly prodded the boy who slumped to the ground. I awoke bathed in sweat, I wanted to call out to Aunt Zindi and thought better. I went to the kitchen for a drink of water and gasped when I saw great-grandfather-in-law sitting in the dark at the kitchen table with his eyes closed. When he heard my movement, his eyes flashed open. His torch-like eyes drilled holes through me as he watched me hurriedly drink a glass of water and scurry out the kitchen.

On the third night the dream played out again like a movie. The man was nowhere. I peered from behind a tree. I stepped closer when I heard a crackling sound. The man was back with a wheelbarrow. He hauled the boy up and flung him into the barrow. He was as limp as a wet rag. Before I could duck back behind the tree, the man looked up right into my eyes, my blood turned to ice — I expected him to run up to attack me. All he did was wheel the dead boy away. To this day I can hear the laboured squeak of the wheelbarrow rolling away.

I waited a week before I told Aunt Zindi about the three-night recurring dream.

Her response was one of frustration, that *here we go again* adult look. She asked me to describe the place in my dream. I thought it odd that she closed her eyes and asked me to repeat the description.

She then shook her head, 'You cannot possibly know the place with such fine detail, you were too young, just eighteen months, to remember what you are recalling.'

I asked a foolish question about why I was having this dream every night and got the answer I deserved.

'Do I look like God to you? How can I know why? You

always ask such questions, you think too much, Jacob. You will go mad if you go on like this!'

She did not stop there she told me to put my thinking to good use and get a good education and a job that will tire me so much, there will be no time for stupid dreams. Did I mention I was sixteen years old?

That was that, she left ranting and raving in a vernacular I did not understand, much to my embarrassment. For years the dream persisted in much the same way, three days in succession and then rewind and begin again for the next cycle of three days.

After the fifth year of the dream sequence, great-grandfather-in-law died. Nobody came to his funeral. Aunt Zindi, my six cousins and I were the only people present. It always baffled me why Aunt Zindi took care of him, he was not her blood relative. She had a big heart is what I put it down to, and perhaps it was the only connection my cousins had to their father. The strange thing is, nobody interacted with him except Aunt Zindi who fed him and washed him.

A week after his death I went to the police station to speak to anyone who would pay attention to my recurring dream. It had eaten into my soul, dream after recurring dream, that I could no longer see it as a dream. It was my reality.

The first policeman I spoke to said, 'Are you on drugs? This makes no sense at all. Don't waste our time, we don't investigate dreams!'

I noticed an older police officer listening in, and he followed me out the building and stopped me on the street. He asked me to repeat what I said to the policeman inside the station. I noted that he was pensive thereafter. He asked me to come over the next day. He wanted to record what I had to say. Two days later he confirmed that there was a murder some fifty years ago in that area, the missing boy's body had washed up from the river, bloated and unrecognizable except for his red shorts. After several sessions with the police officer, an identikit of the dead child and the man I saw in my dreams emerged. He was grateful that I was brave enough to share what seemed to be a bizarre situation. I never told Aunt Zindi that I went to the police. It left me even more unsettled after seeing the identikit of the man — he was familiar, and I did not know why.

In my mid-twenties I studied at the local seminary and joined the ranks of priesthood soon after. I think it was more to heal the spiritual distraction I had with that dream that had plagued me for so many years. It was not as I expected, in taking up the cloth, I thought my union with God would remove the disturbing dreams, but they grew more vivid. It exhausted me every day, and I feared I would fail in my duties. I procrastinated for a long time and finally approached the senior cardinal with my dilemma. He said that I was God's vessel to right the wrongs of the world, that I had to act on all the disturbing dreams I was experiencing. He said I had an inherent sensitivity, and that it chose me as the messenger to report unsolved crimes. This thought left me heavier with the responsibility the cardinal suggested. I knew early on, even before the dreams began that I could see things that others appeared not to see. I had many conversations with my dead mother who appeared before me to encourage me in the growing-up years. Now she did not appear. Premonitions, sensations came with no warning and left me quite depleted. The police department saw me as nothing else but a raving lunatic. The older police officer who gave me a hearing and trusted what I told him, did not give a clear answer on who the man and the boy in the red shorts were. The police officer died and left me with no answers. That he believed me was enough for me to know that I was not insane.

In this land of crime and inhumanity, I feel death every time after reading newspaper reports that state someone is missing, because they do turn up dead soon enough. I had the sight to prevent the crime from happening, but nobody accepted that.

I was wandering the earth carrying this — I saw children being abused, women being mistreated, people murdered for money and the rich abusing the poor. I wandered to those places, hovering outside buildings, praying for the harm not to occur. That was all I could do. Then I wrote letters to the newspaper each time I had a premonition and posted them from various places alerting the public about crimes that were being planned. At first, they ignored my letters. Then newspaper headlines blared, *Phantom Letter Writer — Serial Criminal or Saving Grace?*

Some crimes never happened when they acted upon the details in my letters, but it was hit and miss whether they would catch the perpetrator. It was more important that my letters averted a crime or two.

And this is how I became the letter soothsayer of the city.

AUNT ZINDI WAS NOT PREPARED for the truth that uncovered a family secret emanating from my first dream.

What came to light was that the young boy murdered near the Limpopo River was her great-grandfather-in-law's son, killed by the hands of his own father. The truth of the matter is that it was not his biological son but a child of a politician who knew interracial relationships were forbidden. Great-grandfather-in-law married the girl, as she was then, and unbeknownst to her, she was with child when she married him. Her mother worked as a domestic helper for the politician's family, who like Adam could not look past the forbidden fruit in his home. He contravened his own law making that forbade interracial relationships and left a young girl with a burden she could not hide. Great-grandfather-in-law did not know the boy was not his until a man told him the truth. In a fit of rage, as they thought it, he killed the boy. The truth of his pale skin and light eyes was noticeable when he was out in public with his father. He never spoke to another living soul from that day on, and the boy's mother died from grief in not knowing what had happened to her son.

Last year, Aunt Zindi sold her house to real estate developers. They were excavating the property when they found a locked steel chest that they kindly returned to Aunt Zindi. It was then that she said the chest would have belonged to great-grand-father-in-law as she was living in his house after her husband deserted her and the children to start a new life with a new family.

We gathered at his grave at the Hillfield's cemetery and Aunt Zindi asked me to open the box with her six children present. Two of them and their spouses unlocked the chest.

I prayed over the chest, afraid of what might be inside. A few books and photo albums were near the top. A letter fell out of a book. Aunt Zindi asked me to open it and read it out aloud. I cleared my throat, my hands trembled, and I read the words which stared up at me from a faded page.

You have gathered here to listen to my voice from the grave. Please do not judge me. Now I can tell you the truth about the situation that has labeled me a murderer. Jeremiah could not live a life as a mixed-race child, not in his country. He would have faced terrible times, and I saw it as my duty, although terrible, to save him from such a fate. I am sorry that I had to do this, but it was not out of bitterness that he was not my biological child. I committed a crime punishable with death in a country that kills us off like flies.

I did it because I too, was born a mixed-race child to my unsuspecting mother. A farmer took her innocence which was not his to take. From that woeful act I came into the world. The torment and injustice I faced, not only by the powers of the day, but by my people, family, neighbors. It was intolerable. Being born on neither side of the defined color bar came with untold pressure. We protected Jeremiah as a little boy, but he was growing up and would soon face the harshness I endured. I had to spare him the vice, sin and sorrow of this world. In sparing him, I am wandering in limbo, living the same hell I had on earth, but I set him free.

As I float back into the nether world, please find it in your hearts to forgive me. The prayer on my lips is that you should be free from the suffering of inhumanity.

NONE of us spoke about the letter great-grandfather-in-law wrote after that day. The prayer on my lips is one of forgiveness for him to find peace, and humanity to reign over the world.

OCEANS AWAY

The journey is mapped before we leave

~~~

After a bitter end to twelve years of marriage, Anthea Bliss needed to get away as far as possible to save herself from the harsh glare of those in their common social sphere. Her writing suffered under two years of the strain of court hearings, dividing assets and incessant nastiness. Did they marry for love in the first place or was it a marriage of convenience? These thoughts were never too far in her busy mind. One thing she accepted was that they could never be friends after this — too much had happened for civility to exist between them. The only grace was not having children — she shuddered at what it would have been like to raise a child in the midst of her traumatic, misguided union.

To say he had changed was an untruth. She overlooked the narcissist he was because her heart told a different story. It was over now. She was free to do as she wanted. With a handsome settlement and the family home, a cottage near the river, where they spent the early years of their marriage, she decided that a holiday was what she needed to rekindle her writing mojo. She commissioned an architect to have her writing studio facing the river. This art deco renovation and extension would be ready when she returned from an eighteen night's cruise, and two months roaming around London and Europe to get her creative juices back. She loved a slay of color and the works of Picasso — for once she could have her self-styled space without Stavros breathing down her neck, telling her she did not understand how to use space. As a publisher he held pent-up aggression and unleashed it on Anthea, ten years his junior. He was tired of life and she wanted more from life.

She bought two large brimmed sun hats and heavily shaded sunglasses. Being incognito was the only way to survive. With two cabins booked side by side at the end of the lower deck, she had a balcony to herself and no guests on the other side of her on this luxury cruise liner. Anonymity is what she desired. After two bestsellers and her public divorce she had had enough of society's wagging tongues.

Anthea was a crazy bird, her zany, fun-loving personality always looked to the lighter side of life, yet her writing revealed the dark side of the human heart. Stavros made sure he squashed her need for constant joy. His brooding, serious nature was unappreciative of her bouts of laughter or dancing around the house or singing in the shower. His recurrent comments left her anxious when he said, 'Be quiet, for once, will you?' How could she kill the spirit her parents adored and encouraged? When she lay in her hammock reading for hours at their river-side cottage, he called her idle and lazy — never thinking, he thought her incapable of using her brain to any good use. His staff tolerated but disliked him at the Publishing House on the East side of town. In his mid-fifties he was older in his rejection of joy and hope. His increasing negativity hurt her creative energy, the endless criticisms and need to tell her what she should write and how she should write it exhausted her until she stopped — two years and nothing. Somehow after the break-up, she found the determination to regain the pleasure and passion that he took from her. When she gave up, he knew it, everything went downhill, and mutual friends blamed her for ending their union. Yet, they knew his horrid tendency to put her down in company, making her the object of his bitter ridicule while courting attention for how wonderful he was.

Eighteen days of bliss away from people she knew. The sea beckoned, and she answered with an extravagant holiday alone before she returned to her refurbished writing studio. Healing her tattered soul and energising her creative spirit was a mission she hoped to achieve.

Her step was lighter that morning when she boarded the ship. The passengers appeared to be in their mid-forties and older, much to her relief. They might pursue sedate activities in casting aside the thrills of everyday life and she could revisit her muse in peace. Money was not an issue — she could spend it as she pleased, she would claim every indulgence as and when it arose. Solitude and privacy were high on her agenda, booking two cabins for complete solitude was her way of claiming this.

The first night on board, she ordered a room service dinner — she planned to decompress with lots of sleep, binge watching movies if she chose to, and reading to her heart's content. She decided she would be lazy — she earned the title from her ex-husband and now that she was running her own ship, it did not matter anymore whether he thought her a waste of space.

After a luxurious soak in the gigantic oval bathtub, she fell asleep with the DVD player whirring in the background. Anthea woke up with a start around 11:30 pm. She dashed to the bath-room, hit her shoulder against the wall, then realized she was not at home, the bathroom was on the other side of the cabin. It was black out on the balcony, not a star in the sky, the ship was on steady waters bobbing in a gentle cradle rock — she had no idea how far they had traveled or where she was. She stepped out and inhaled the cool salty air, it stung her nostrils. A walk on the upper deck appealed to her at this hour, she donned a light tracksuit, a pair of runners and headed up. Nobody was out and about at that hour. She assumed sedate passengers had retired for the night to the soothing sound of the sea.

She veered towards the left of the deck — the pub up ahead was dimly lit. A quick look inside when she got close revealed a lone male figure bending over his drink with his back facing her. He was the only person in the bar. From behind the shadow of a pillar she observed him — observing human behaviour was her job after all, and her psychology training gave her the advantage of speculation in judging body language. She concluded he was a tad unhappy therefore drowning his sorrows in a drink alone in a bar. Nobody she knew had ever gone on a cruise vacation alone, save for her. Was he too running away from something? It tickled her curiosity. She watched him for quite a while as he ordered a second drink. The waiter's deadpan look suggested the man must have been in the bar for the entirety of the evening. Then he turned around, she dived out of view thinking he might have seen her cowering in the strip of light reflected from the bar. Under the obscure lighting he looked like he was in his fifties, a man with an olive tan, an exotic looking handsome man with his shiny black hair right out of the movie *Casablanca* until she noticed his ponytail. Her imagination kicked into overdrive now, could he be an artist, perhaps a painter, a musician? It was hard to tell from that distance. This lone, mystery figure intrigued her. With fifteen crime fiction books under the name, A L Tenebris, she took the 'L' from her paternal great-grandmother, 'Louise' whom she had not met in the living world — now she had the impending desire to craft the man's world. She suddenly realized, lost in a maze of thoughts, that he was heading for the exit. She dashed down the opposite side of the boat to get back to her cabin. Opting for the stairs at the last minute and pacing up her step to get ahead was not such a good idea. She heard heavy footsteps behind her. With her head bent low to conceal her face she felt a swish of air encircle her as the man rushed past. A soft voice said, 'Good night, Ms Tenebris.' Anthea hesitated, rigid, unable to respond. Her cover was blown, he walked ahead without flinching — his flapping ponytail confirmed he was the mystery man from the bar. How did he know her pen name? She caught a quick sideview glimpse of his thin strip of beard lining his angular jaw. In that moment she imagined he was a famous artist and then tossed the idea out in fear of how he knew who she was.

She grabbed her journal when she returned to her cabin, writing everything that tumbled out of her head.

Who is he? Why is he alone? What nationality is he? I'll name him 'Pedro.' Has he been sent to follow me?

She went to bed, without her earphones as she usually did to listen to binaural dreaming music. The gentle sound of the sea lapped up against the side of the ship like a content slurping cat, the rhythmic sound soothed her.

The jarring telephone woke her earlier than she was ready to rise. A gentle French voice greeted her on the other end of the line. Her first thought was, is it him? How did he find me? The voice explained that he was calling from room service. They had her breakfast order, but she had not ticked the delivery time. She apologized and asked if she could have her breakfast in half an hour.

'Yes, that will be possible, is there anything else Madame would like this morning?'

'That will be all, thank you, I'm sorry for the mix-up.'

'Not to worry Madame. We did not want to disturb you if you were not ready, that is all.'

No sooner had she put down the telephone, she called back.

'Please leave my breakfast at the door and ring the bell to alert me, I might be in the shower,' she lied, not wanting to face anyone that morning.

'No problem, I will, Madame.'

An hour later when the doorbell rang, she waited to hear footsteps departing along the wooden floor before she opened the door and pulled in the food trolley. She picked up the *Reader's Digest* that was placed next to the coffeepot. How wonderful that she received the magazine with her breakfast. She flicked through the pages deciding which article to read first. Waffles had never been her breakfast choice in her former life, she tossed aside her usual poached eggs and smoked salmon for a sweet breakfast. Pizza the night before, waffles, fruit and cream this morning was not like her at all. She laughed aloud when a silly vision floated into head of her squeezing out the cabin door after eighteen days of indulgent eating. More brisk walks had to be scheduled into her day. Cabin space was limited, not adequate for stretching or doing a few Zumba moves. Her eye caught an article titled, *Surviving A Marriage Break-up* — she tossed the magazine onto the bed.

The sky was a brilliant blue that morning with the sun circled by a haze of mingled colors, high overhead. Her urge to walk on the upper deck to look out over the horizon from that vantage point was tempting. She grabbed her broad, floppy hat, sunglasses, a tube of sunblock, and a book, leaving the *Reader's Digest* behind as she raced to the top.

People lazed about on the deck taking in the warmth and views. Recliners with women in bikinis and men in shorts, reading or lying face down while their partners' rubbed oil on their warm backs was a teasing sensual sight. Cool air wafted around her with the aroma of salt air mixed with lavender oil. This combination of smells made her queasy. Stavros hated her persistent clearing of smells in the house. He said she had the nose of a dog, smelling things that human noses could not detect. She shook her head to forget those days. One recliner was vacant two seats away from her. She thought of changing her seat when she saw a pair of large flat feet walk towards it, then long lanky legs at first until her eyes moved up to a lean torso and then she saw his face, an unmistakable Cary Grant lookalike — she looked away before he caught sight of her — both wore heavy shaded sunglasses. He must have sensitive eyes she thought, and poked her nose back in her book. He was too close for her people watching today. It was a waste of time trying to read, her mind lingered on the man. She questioned herself — why am I so keen to know who he is? Perhaps it's my muse telling me to pursue the story. She glanced his way, peering between the colored cocktail glasses making sure her head was not too noticeable under her floppy hat. He appeared to be asleep. She left to get back to her journal.

She giggled and twirled around her cabin, thinking — I have a story!

A spot of browsing around the onboard designer shops filled her afternoon, she decided to spoil herself with a piece of jewellery and wandered into the store. A couple was poring over a tray of rings with a smiling attentive salesperson groveling around them. When Anthea heard a male voice with a transatlantic accent say, 'We'll take this one, thanks,' she glanced over into the eyes of the mystery man. The lady with him had her back to her, she had short red hair. She was silent on their way out the store. He put his arm around her and glanced back at Anthea. The hair on her arms and neck rose with the intensity of his look. She waited for the couple to be out of sight before she left to purchase a pair of sandals for an onshore trip scheduled the next day. Mystery man is not alone, she surmised.

The ship docked at Falmouth. Andrea was excited about wandering around deciding where she would have a leisurely lunch when she caught a glimpse of mystery man bent over in conversation with a woman at the coffee shop across the street. Something about this man mesmerised her, she stopped to watch him. He was caressing the arm of the woman and reached out to kiss her hand. She was a much younger woman and blonde, to boot! Not the red-haired woman she saw him with the day before! Well, what do you know, mystery man has a secret! He looked up and nodded, acknowledging seeing her again. She spun around, the left strap on her new sandal snapped when a loose stone hooked onto it. He grinned at the amusing sight of her hobbling away with her sandal tucked under her arm. A sickening feeling ran through her as she wondered how much longer before he approached her. She headed a distance away to an unobtrusive café for lunch. Her select dining hopes were dashed.

She had fifteen days on board, so she might bump into him again unless she stayed locked in her cabin. He had an uncanny way of being wherever she was. She bunkered down for three days of frenetic writing, ordering in her meals and writing like one beset by a thousand crazed muses. Drama on the high seas consumed her... a wife... another woman... a man with secrets on board a luxury ship. What outcome would she give him? Carbohydrate dense meals left her drained, she needed air and a walk, her knees and back ached from crouching over her journal.

It was threatening to rain, she grabbed a scarf and rain jacket and headed to a deserted upper deck. She leaned on the railings and looked out as far as her eye could see into the rapidly diminishing, foggy horizon. Anthea took several deep breaths and a few brisk laps around the deck and returned to the look-out point. Her energy levels were pumped. She returned refreshed to her cabin to pick up her writing. When she marched towards the desk, she realized her journal was not there. She rummaged through the desk and her bag, no journal! For the life of her she could remember nothing, other than leaving it on the desk to head out for a walk. She called housekeeping to ask if they had cleaned the room in her absence.

'No Madame, you ordered a cocktail and when we went to deliver it, the *Do not disturb* sign was on your door. We did not want to ring the bell and returned with your drink. Would you like us to bring it up to you, Madame?'

'No, please cancel that order, I'm so sorry for being a nuisance.'

This time the telephone clicked down on her with no assurances that she was not a nuisance.

The tension in her neck increased, she was sure she didn't

take the journal out on deck with her, or did she? It confused her why she could not remember ordering a cocktail. She put it down to her writing frenzy and overactive imagination that had to be checked.

Nobody knew where she was, nobody cared, she had no one to talk to — isolation crept back. How could she not remember where she put her journal? She felt her breathing tighten, and she needed to be outdoors again. Stress brought on these panic attacks, she had to stop it before it overpowered her — she had to get out. With a jumper drawn across her shoulders, she hurried back to the upper deck. She stretched and touched her toes, moved her head from left to right, hoping to ease the tension in her neck. As she leaned over the railing a warm hand touched her shoulder. Her neck tightened, who was this behind her? Then she heard the voice say, 'Are you following me, or, am I following you?'

She turned around to his hot breath on her face, she felt light-headed, ready to swoon with the smell of spent tobacco flooding her nostrils.

'I don't know what you mean,' she slurred.

'It's simple,' he laughed, '*You, are* following me.'

From somewhere in the depths of her soul she summoned the courage.

'I can't see how people won't bump into each other all the time in this space, so what you're saying makes little sense.' Irritation gave her strength as it did with Stavros.

'Interesting,' is all he said.

'Please step aside, I need to get back to my cabin.'

He leered at her, still too close, then he smiled, revealing a black hole in the front of his mouth and a glinting gold tooth next to it. She pushed past him and headed for the stairs. All romantic notions died in that moment — he was no artist!

'Good night, sleep well!' His laugh sent a spine-chilling vibration through her.

She stopped dead in her tracks at her cabin door, drenched

with perspiration and a maddening palpitating in her chest when she saw a *Do not Disturb* sign on her door. How did it get there if she did not put it out? She flung the door open and threw herself on the bed. Her head clanged with a barrage of confused thoughts. Why was she going through this? All she wanted was space, not intrusions into her life from strangers. She looked across at the desk and jumped up — the journal was back where she had left it!

She opened it. Inside sat a complete typed manuscript, with the title *Stranger At Sea,* and someone had ripped out all her handwritten pages! The room spun, forcing her to sit down. She opened the manuscript and read it. The words were not as she had written them. Someone changed every page. It was her story, edited and corrected by a stranger — a stranger at sea.

She must have fallen asleep. The sun streamed onto her face from the open balcony door. She saw an envelope under the door, on her way to the bathroom. With trembling hands, she picked it up. The words burned a hole in her head.

It read:

If you publish your book, be sure to include your co-writer's name. The name is:

Pedro Deville

She arrived home far more exhausted than when she left.

She picked up the phone to set up a meeting with her agent on the new story she had co-ghost written oceans away.

FINAL VIEW

The dignity of life lives in death

~~~~

I worked most nights through to the morning at the funeral parlour, washing, dressing, and beautifying ladies who died either peacefully or tragically. Families entrusted their beloved to my final care. I had to prepare them for the day of family viewing, and the funeral day. The eyes of the living world would be cast on the deceased's face, some might say, 'She looks so lovely, so peaceful,' with a tear in the eye, others perhaps, 'Poor woman, she struggled, you know,' and more would utter compliments on the contributions the departed made to the world and then again others would gossip about a few untold secrets.

My friends could never understand why I was a mortician. Their unkind voices rang in my ears for many years. 'What a macabre profession! Could you not find any other job?' and 'Angelica, this is a joke, right, you surely can't be serious!' Undeterred by these harsh comments and expectations about what I should and couldn't do from my closest friends, hurt, but the people who mattered, my family, respected my choice.

I pursued a course of study that earned me an associate degree in Mortuary Science. I am on call twenty-fours of the day. Death comes, most often when unexpected. For me it's not only about arranging and conducting the funeral, a major part of this role is also comforting grieving families which I prioritise. It's a multifaceted role, and hey, somebody has to do it, so why all the exclamations and protests from supposed friends? It is a necessary and delicate aspect of life and living, yes, living. It is the end stop of our existence when we can no longer do it for ourselves in this world and a trusted person is required to conduct the send-off in a respectful and dignified way. Those friends left the friendship fold, and I got over them.

Are you wondering why I am a mortician as opposed to anything else? I'll tell you because I got asked this question a lot in the earlier years, and you kindly did not ask.

There are two reasons. One stemmed from seeing my grandmother die — a beautiful soul with the smile and eyes of a loving angel. Her lovely round face gave her a child-like look and a smile that drew others to return for her warmth, especially after a bad day. She wore no make-up, a natural beauty she was. A dash of moisturiser during the day, but an intense cleansing regime at night was her beauty routine. Her full lips had a hint of lip balm — that was all. She smelt delicious. I loved snuggling up to her and being cradled on her lap. My unforgettable, beautiful Nan, a calm and loving magnet for all her grandchildren, I liked to think I had a special place in her heart. The thing is, at her funeral, when my father picked me up to have a peek at her beautiful face in the coffin, I smiled in anticipation, eager to see her face again, but alas it was not the Nan I knew and loved.

They removed her body from our home, and we had to wait two weeks for the funeral. My father's brother who lived in Switzerland wanted to be there to bury Nan. I remember the day she died as clear as day. She sat out in the backyard reading. Nan loved romance novels and spent hours lost in the pages of her books. She read with her eyebrows ever so arched and her eyes misty which made me want to read her books. She sensed my eagerness to know what she read, 'This is not for your heart and brain just yet, Angelica. When you are older, then you can be swept away as I am when I read these stories, not now.' I wanted to be swept away, I wanted to grow up quickly to lose myself inside the pages of the books that gave my Nan such pleasure. She nursed a cold that week and took in the sun's warmth that morning. I went to get her a glass of water after a bout of coughing. When I returned, she was asleep. The smile on her face glowed with peace. I lifted the book out of her hands, half expecting her to open her eyes, ready to tell me, I could not read her book now. Instead she slipped lower in the seat and the hand that held her book, dropped and dangled to the side of the chair. She was so still I ran into the house to let my father know. I called out to him. He enjoyed a leisurely Sunday morning shower and was humming some old tune with the shower at full throttle that I had to bang on the door before he heard me.

'Dad, come quickly, I think Nan is not well, she's not moving.'

'I'll be out there soon, stay with her, don't panic.'

Dad called the doctor when Nan remained unresponsive. He said she had passed. She looked so peaceful I couldn't believe the doctor. The centre of my world was no longer there. Nan was gone. I was in a daze for a few days, believing it was all a mistake and that she would be back soon.

The first family viewing of her beautiful face, as I said, was not as I had expected.

I peered into the box, all I saw was a ghostly white, powdered face and stark red lips outlined in black! The person lying before me was not my Nan.

'That's not Nan, who is this?'

My father felt me tense and patted my arm to avoid my raised anxiety distressing my aunts.

'It is Nan, darling, they've put a lot of make-up on her to make her look pretty that's all.'

'She was pretty as she was, no it's not her.'

My father understood my pain and said nothing more. Later my aunts spoke in lowered voices outside the chapel, trying to avoid being overheard with family and friends within earshot.

'Who chose this mortician? They've done a bad job with mum. It's not at all like her.'

'We can't blame Fred. He did the best he could while we were distraught. He had to do what he had to do.'

'Surely they should have asked for photographs or asked to speak to one of us, you would think.'

At eight years old, this left an indelible impression.

Did I mention that my father worked at the forensic department? He had uncovered details on difficult cases that were left unresolved for many years. It brought him some notoriety. He had many radio and newspaper interviews locally and abroad. He was not after fame, just passionate about his work. My father was a workaholic, often working late at night, at home, bringing photographs with him that he would analyse, and shape a narrative around. He worked on the physical aspects at the laboratory.

As an only child, I moved around adult conversations unless forbidden to do so and was sent to bed earlier than most children my age. My father told me to stay upstairs, in my bedroom, when he worked in his basement office. Need I say more, the forbidden invited a greater curiosity — they prohibited me from any knowledge of the case, and I wanted to know more, simple. Any psychologist will tell you it was normal, that I was not a bad kid. While it absorbed my father for many hours late into the night, I peered through the crack in the door. I remember hearing my father's telephone conversations with his work colleagues on some murder cases, and sometimes he would chat to Nan about his work — she made sure I was in bed before she had those chats with him. I would creep out of bed and sit at the top of the stairs listening to them talk downstairs. They discussed murders and child molestations, unpalatable subjects for a child's ears. I had the stamina for it, never having night-mares except that I was wide-eyed, all night long thinking about those poor people who died, or were abused, and the cruelty of those who perpetrated the crimes. It's a wonder that I didn't become a crime fiction writer or detective! While my father worked, I saw faces pinned on his cork board, the before and after shots — gruesome findings. Sometimes he worked with an artist to reconstruct details of the deceased's face, giving them back their sense of identity — the DNA, blood, skin, bone and teeth business, dad worked on at the laboratory during the day. I did my private sketches from the bits I picked up. I hid them from Nan and my father for fear they would tighten the already strict house rules for curious little girls. Sometimes my father had to attend court hearings to provide his findings. How I wanted to listen in during those days. I should be thankful I was not scarred by this.

Now you know what led to my choice to be a mortician.

I wanted to restore dignity and authenticity in death. I trained my staff in my parlor to put compassion first in helping families process their grief. Compassion was our top value, followed by respect and reverence for the deceased and their loved ones. They released no person without my final go-ahead — nobody would endure what my family and I experienced with Nan's passing. We scoured through photographs for the most authentic understanding of who the departed was, in a visual sense, in the living years. We collaborated with the fami-lies, if they wanted to be present during the preparatory phase before the funeral, we allowed them that right. I was hard with staff who disregarded my parlor rules and civil expectations, if I had to let them go, I did so without overthinking the decision.

Like the birth of a baby brings much joy to a family, and is treated with delicate care and respect, so too was my view on how death should be revered. The entry and departure from this earthly plane had to be equal. When it came to the day of the funeral, I always did the introductory funeral speech, but we were increasingly in high demand because of our respect and compassion — highly prized human values in any walk of life. It was physically impossible for me to do this on my own with the high volume of work. It was a blessing when my niece joined me. Now we were a family business. It was her choice to come on board. She had a remarkable eye for detail and understood pain after having lost a child herself in a tragic accident. People asked for her, her compassion and soft touch were an elixir to their grief. She mentored younger staff and kept the mission statement alive at the parlor. She added an extension to the role by enquiring on the likes and dislikes of the departed, down to their taste in music. My niece played this at the parlor while we dressed and prepared the deceased for the final viewing and their last rites. She never shied away from talking to the departed as if they were actively listening to her. It was her connection to the spirit world as the comfort to a soul who might not yet have settled and could well be floating in limbo.

The job is emotionally draining, as you serve first and never take time to process how you are feeling. In the early days, I sought counseling to deal with the grief of others that I faced daily. Now we have in-house therapists to help staff cope, to allow them to have the emotional capacity for themselves and their families. We ran meditation sessions to help staff gather themselves on difficult days to allow them to remain intact at home. Religious organizations work with us to ensure we respect culture and last rites matters. Death's door does not discriminate, it levels us in dust or ash. Life segments people. Grief binds us together — angst is a universally shared aspect of living. We work side by side in death, living the grief of all who enter our parlor doors. Care is our promise, how can anyone fake that, it's not clinical, the only clinical part of my job is storing the body, the encasement, I call it. Preserving is immediate because decay is rapid. Doctors, first response trauma agencies, all face a similar fate when caring for victims. Altruism is an innate reaction, if denied, it leads to, or occurs as a psychological issue.

I remember my conversation, several conversations with a young intern afraid to be alone in a room with the departed. I gave her all the reasons we should fear the living more than the dead. After all was it not Shakespeare who said, *Hell is empty, and all the devils are here.* I provided examples from the cases my father had worked on. Soon she was my second in charge working alongside my niece. We must keep the spirit, I mean, the departed personality alive for family members, to help ease their pain. My staff is a superb lot at knowing just how to do that, by either quoting the humor or contributions of loved ones, who were no longer with them.

Nan's funeral day was hellish for me, but I shelved it by remembering the joy in her smile, loving eyes when she spoke to me and her misty eyes while reading. That got me through the rest of my childhood with my father's help. I would be lying if I said I have a dry eye when I remember Nan, but it is a tear of love, not deep-felt sadness.

I AM NINETY-ONE TODAY, the reality of death is close at hand. I have lived and served as and how I wanted. I am blessed to have a lucid mind. Who is lucky enough to plan their own final viewing? I got my niece to freshen up my red silk scarf and booked my manicurist to ensure that both my fingernails and toenails were painted the same color. Lord knows who you will meet along the eternal way! Now when I enter the pearly gates, I want to be as I am in life, someone who arrives just the way she left.

In life and in death we are the same. I want them to say up there, I know I'm going up, something tells me that, and I will hear the melody in, 'Open the way, Angelica's arrived! She sure looks fine!'

THE CALL OF THE OUTBACK

Home is the umbilical yearning

~~~

The burnt-out car lurked in the tall grass that only the wind could expose. Rusty, alone, forgotten in secrets and shame.

Inspector Donovan had retired from the force. He bought a camper van and took to the road for some alone time as he set out across the outback, just him and the sounds of nature — far away from dense civilization to rekindle the magical years of his youth. The open road, reckless abandonment and being accountable to no one was the life he treasured.

One morning he pulled up the trailer on the side of a dirt track, much in need of a long walk through the bush after long stretches of driving, with a few snatched catnaps here and there. A tramp through the bush always refreshed him, gave him a new perspective as a teenager when life tossed him a few challenges. Now, mature contemplation in the heart of nature was the bliss of retirement after a long and illustrious career in the city, heading a busy police precinct.

He was grateful for the half-esky, half-backpack with chilled beers and fresh fruit, water and ham sandwiches to sustain him. The burn of the sun on his skin and the wind through the last sprigs of hair on his patchy head was his freedom from the smog, deception and cruelty he witnessed in the big smoke — now all that was behind him. He walked away happy that he had the blessing of good health to catch a few more years of the joy of youth. He marked his way as he walked, to trace his steps back to the camper van later that day. The further in he walked the less evidence there was that human feet had walked that way. He trudged on for almost two hours before he settled down for lunch under a clump of eucalyptus trees. Up in the trees, koalas hung onto branches, drunk with sleep. They looked at him in slow motion with eyelids that rose, half-blinked and closed in dreaminess.

'That's the way guys, you know how to live!' he laughed, 'I need some of that sleep fellas, so no disturbance.'

Donovan loved the Australian fauna and flora, it was in his blood, his birthright to the soil. The city never elicited the ease he felt in the bush. He counted the days to retirement in his last years at the force. He leaned back against the tree, pulled his outback hat over his face and drifted off to the sound of dehydrated buzzing flies searching for a quencher. An orchestra of human snoring and buzzing flies were the only sounds heard as rotund koalas slumbered in a hypnotic daze. God's country was raw in its natural state just as Donovan knew it. He grew up on his family's barley and wheat farm amidst rolling grasslands for as far as the eye could see in heat and dust.

Years spent in the force in Sydney governed by fast lifestyles and gruesome crimes reflected the dark side that city life bred. The dark side of the bush brought fires, floods and red dust storms. The police force attracted his entry into the metropolis —

he spent his youth reading detective fiction until he felt the tug of bright lights, police sirens and the allure of an adrenaline rush in saving lives and solving crimes. The hectic years of blood, gore and evil passed by with no time to nurture his emotional needs. Relationships never lasted, so he opted for a life alone. He was no heartbreaker, but his job consumed him, leaving no space to sustain a long-term relationship.

He remained happily single.

AN HOUR later he woke to a breeze fluttering through the trees. He looked up, the koalas resettled their positions and slumped over again. What a bloody brilliant life he thought, to be able to waft from one sleep to the next with not a care in the world. He felt a kinship with the little fellas and knew that every cop in his precinct would trade places with him if they could. Their lives were endless nights of wakefulness drowning in barrel loads of strong coffee. Stake outs, briefings, interviewing neighborhoods, convening line-ups and facing criminals in whatever situations arose. The demands of the force stamped sleepless nights on their foreheads. They were grumpy and distant.

Donovan stood up, stretched, touched his toes and slowly eased his back. An old hip injury left him with a twinge every time he slept or sat for too long in one position. He took a bullet in the hip in a drug related siege situation. He reached for the Tiger balm and rubbed some into his left hip. The burn eased the stiffness faster than any other balm. He walked back to his camper van with a slower step.

Crows circled overhead and swooped down around him, curious about this foreigner in their space. He pushed his bag of beef jerky back into his pocket. Chewing was his way to relaxation and deep thoughts. The crows were a tad too close and likely to peck him for the jerky. The scarecrow on his parents' property, that he fondly named 'Old Joe' was a victim of the crows over the years, but his mother never left Old Joe's head and shirt tattered for too long, she fixed it like a mother would tend a child. Donovan had no intention of ending up tattered like 'Old Joe,' for a piece of jerky that would be ripped from his hands.

The wind picked up, and the crows disappeared. He raised his head, looked across the long grass that swished, twirling in a crazed dancing gyration. A speck of something in the horizon caught his eye as the grass parted. He pulled out his binoculars for a closer view. With the next big gust of wind, the grass parted to reveal the hood of an abandoned vehicle. His fascination kicked in like the crows swooping over a foreign presence in a desolate, forgotten place. With a quickened pace it was soon revealed that the vehicle, a Chrysler Valiant, was a burnt-out ruin. Donovan circled the vehicle a few times. This was his habit at the force until he gained a skeletal sense of what might have transpired at a crime scene. The vehicle appeared to have been there for a long time. It had partially sunk into the ground up to the bottom of the doors, enough was visible above ground, spookily, as if it wanted to be found.

Donovan froze when he saw the blackened, rusty, misshapen frame of a baby seat, facing the rear of the vehicle. He shuddered at the thought that an infant might have died in the car. He then consoled himself that perhaps the child was not in the vehicle when it went up in flames. He questioned whether anyone would have survived the blaze, or worse still, did someone set it alight with the passengers inside! Instinctively he knew he had to take photographs of this find to pass on to police headquarters. The compact Nikon Colpix camera was a godsend gift from the ladies at the force. He clicked a few photographs on the Nikon, some on his iPhone and did a short video of the location. He sent the photographs to his mate at the Sydney police station. The red exclamation mark annoyed him. There was no mobile connection. Once he stepped away from the car, his phone picked up service and the photographs flew off into cyberspace bringing the abandoned Chrysler Valiant back to life. What disturbed Donovan was why the car had been undetected for so many years. Restlessness stole his tranquility for the first time in the bush. His phone beeped in acknowledgement that his photographs had arrived and were sent to the station closest to his current location. He studied the mangled mess creating scenarios in his head about what might have happened. Nothing made sense.

When he got back to his camper van, he had a call from Sydney telling him someone was coming out to see him in the morning and he was to remain there overnight. The request was to pass on his mobile number and vehicle registration. For a second Donovan had the terrifying thought that local police might perceive him as the criminal. How was it possible that he stumbled upon this decade ago situation? He drove to a clearing further along the way and pulled up for the night. Nobody would attack him at night, there was no human presence in this empty expanse. No vehicles were on this dirt track. It was a long way off from the main road.

He tossed and turned that night with the unsettled dreams of years at the force.

The next morning he made himself a hearty breakfast of fried eggs and bacon and his favorite brew of filtered coffee. The frozen bread rolls thawed overnight and were baking to a crisp perfection when he heard a vigorous knocking at the front of the camper van.

'Mr Donovan, Mr Donovan! Inspector? Holmes, here, from Scarborough Village police station.'

Donovan opened the side door of the camper van to the round smiling face of a tanned police officer whose gleaming boots were untouched by the red dust outside.

'There's a heavenly aroma wafting all over the countryside!' Holmes laughed.

'Thank you for coming out, may I pour you a mug of coffee?'

'Could not refuse that, Mr Donovan, and if it's not too much to ask, I would love one of your hot bread rolls, that butter sinking in makes it hard to resist.'

'May I fry you some eggs to go with the bacon and bread rolls?'

'Just the bread will do me good, thank you,' he chuckled.

He couldn't remember anyone as jolly as Holmes at the force he served. Grumpy, complaining men who hated their jobs greeted him every day. Heading the precinct was difficult when staff lacked passion.

'Nifty setup you have here, Mr Donovan, very nice, indeed! I would so love to take to the road when I retire, get up in a new place every morning. What a life!'

'Well, you must drive yourself to a new place every day to wake up there,' Donovan laughed.

'True, true. Now after a quick chat on your discovery yesterday, I'm heading over to the location. Care to join me?'

'What do you make of what might have happened that led to the vehicle being abandoned in the middle of nowhere?'

'Can't be certain just yet, although my head of department went over to chat with a previous station commander who is in a nursing home these days. Some interesting details came up but are yet to be verified.'

'Oh, may I know what information you received, that is if it's not classified stuff?'

'No, not classified. We don't have a case yet. The old guy said a family, a young family went missing around the mid to late sixties, after someone found a young drover dead on their property. They never returned. People speculated that they might have left the country, who knows?'

'Interesting that you should say young family. There's a baby seat in the car.' Donovan was eager to get to the bottom of what happened. Thoughts of retirement flew out into the breeze as he got into Holmes' jeep for a drive back to the abandoned vehicle. 'This might be an unsolved murder or murders, perhaps.' He scratched his chin, his usual habit when trying to understand something.

'Glad to have you along with me. Legend has it that you were quite the leader at the force in the city. From what I heard you solved some pretty tough cases.'

Donovan smiled and said nothing until he felt confused about the track they took.

'Can you please stop? I need to get out to get my bearings. Holmes stopped — the minute Donovan's foot hit the ground he knew they should veer to the left. The eucalyptus trees were in that direction.

The burnt-out vehicle was as he saw it yesterday, a hidden presence, silent, secretive and waiting.

'Yes, this has been here for a long time. It's clear up close although your photographs were excellent.' Holmes videoed the scene as he narrated what he saw and thought about the finding. When Donovan asked about a child being in the vehicle, Holmes said he had a folder in the jeep on the missing family that the ex-station head had mentioned.

'Do you have time to read through the notes?'

'I do, but I need to be in the next town by six o'clock tonight to catch the schnitzel dinner at a pub there. Best in the country I hear. Now you know why I must take long walks in the bush, or I won't fit in the camper van.' Both men shared a bellow of laughter sending two red-capped robins flitting away.

'One life Mr Donovan, we have just one life, enjoy it!' Holmes was in his late forties, born and raised in the city. He married a bush girl and moved there from the city.

Donovan read through the notes — a young couple, Jeffery and Suzette Jones, who owned a sheep station had taken on a casual drover from Western Australia and had him stay on as Jeffery enjoyed his company. He lived in the room above the barn. The young drover found dead in the barn, had a gash at the back of his head. The bloodied crowbar was beside his body.

The perpetrator left in a hurry. Jeffery and Suzette Jones disappeared, and nobody knew what had happened to them.

'This is fascinating information. Look if you need a helping hand, I'm happy to stick around for a few days to assist. Just tell me where to park off my van and I'm your man.'

'That will be great! I could use your expertise on cold cases around here. You can park on my property and Mariette and I will be happy to have you as our guest. The kids have all left. As soon as they turned eighteen, they headed to Sydney. Our nest is empty, so you are most welcome to stay at the house.'

'You are kind, thank you, but I prefer to stay over in the van, it's got my whole life in there. Hope you don't mind, Holmes. Look I don't know that I can stay on, but this situation has intrigued me, I'm happy to help on that.'

'Whatever will keep you around is fine by me, mate.'

WHAT HE SCHEDULED to be a few days, ended up being three weeks in Scarborough Village. Lots came to light on the events that triggered the death of the young drover. An elderly neighbor who knew Jeffrey as a little boy said he had a volatile temper. She revealed what came to her ears as neighborly gossip. The Jones's had a three-month-old baby girl that brought them great joy. One night, Jeffrey returned from a meeting in the next town to find the drover in the house carrying his baby girl and leaning in close to Suzette. She was unaware that Jeffrey had arrived and was watching them through the verandah window. That intimate little scene set him off, and an argument ensued between husband and alleged lover boy. The woman who helped Suzette with the house and the baby told a neighbor what had happened. Both never reported what they knew to the police. Suzette Jones' helper had since died leaving the now elderly neighbor holding the key to the secret of the abandoned farm and burnt-out vehicle. Speculation had it that perhaps

Jeffrey set the car alight killing them all. He knew the land well and would have known where the vehicle would go undetected.

Donovan stayed on in Scarborough Village helping Holmes from time to time and hit the road whenever the wind called out to him.

THOSE WERE THE DAYS

Justice comes in its own time

~~~

I remember those days — carefree, cruel and enlightening.
Leaving the sheltered family fold was difficult. Well, I
saw it that way although I returned home every month for
a weekend. Barely eighteen, never having ventured anywhere on
my own apart from going to school, the local bookstores and
library, that was the sum of my trips without the family. Now
here I was, bright-eyed and ready to take on the year as a full-
time college student, but little did I know that it was to be a year
of life lessons that the application forms neglected to include.
Lessons that went beyond the covers and pages of any book I
had ever read or would read that year.

The university residence, the hostel or digs as some might
call it, came with its own problems. The joy was the endless days
and nights with friends. A shared room with a close friend from
high school, and a corridor of high school mates, attests to the
limited tertiary institutions available... let's say to certain people

of a particular hue. Ahem, I say that with a level of irritation. The togetherness was good. It was fun. We worked hard. We had big dreams. The world of study was a promising oyster, and we were out to get as many of those pearls of wisdom to enfranchise ourselves.

Like I said there were life lessons.

Sheltered, cocooned, locked away, the past — not perceived as a year of living dangerously. Oh no that was never imagined.

The dreaded night of initiation into campus life was inescapable if you were a hostel resident. New student angst, perhaps, it depends on how you look at it. Anxiety gripped all doe-eyed first years — some were a crying mess after hearing horror stories from predecessors. And did they lay it on thick and nasty — they sure did! Introverts cowered in the background, the bold and brazen, few among us, were the first to be noticed and mocked — asked to crawl on all fours, beg, snivel and cry. If you were lucky, you got to table dance and sing a few nursery rhymes. But, if you lacked rhythm there was a round of crawling and crying added to the list of activities, before you were inducted into the hall of acceptance. To a student who had not left the confines of home, it was a baptism by fire — it is laughable now, there was no physical harm, but humiliation and embarrassment rehearsed and served to sickening perfection. Some initiation maestros were students for life at the campus, the perennial, forever seniors, delighting in making newcomers endure the shame they felt decades earlier — now they were permanent residents who squandered their parents' money for their perverse jollies! Yawn. Now I say, get a life! Back then, you got it — I was a sniveling mess when I realized that the world had a few nasties.

Then there was Friday lunch, institution lunch. You know people in prison or hospital wait for the day their favorite dish is served because all else is nauseating. Friday was fish and chips day. I have an aversion in the latter years for beer battered fish, but back then it was the food of the gods, except for the tomato sauce. Something nasty, it sure was. It tasted like it had been thinned down with a barrel of vinegar. Gag factor personified! The problem with Friday lunch was not just restricted to the tomato sauce, but, if you had a lecture near the main hall, you had to walk all the way, a long way, across campus to the fish and chips. Then it was cold — have you eaten beer battered fish that is cold? Rigor mortis sets in that no amount of mastication can rectify! Hence the aversion these days, you see. You had to cut class to make sure you got some of that fish before it was out at sea with not a fried fin in sight. Students, universally are a hungry lot and will do anything, like Oliver Twist for more.

Those were the days. A one-plate portable stove was a godsend on those 'missed meals' days. A can of fish, an onion and tomato made a small meal a taste of home when a dash of chili was thrown into the bubbling sauce. They were tasters really, not a meal, for seven starving students who ate too much popcorn to fill the gap. We relished the company in those days as we crowded around a cooking pot, inhaling the aroma of canned fish like it was a banquet, and laughing so much that hunger pangs evaporated in the tiny steam-filled dorm room. Magical days, indeed! I have never felt such joy again — ah, the simple pleasures of life return in unforgettable memories of a carefree, sweet time.

As first-year intakes, there was a curfew in place and a matron who ensured missing in action students had a few stripes removed. A matron, can you believe it? It was an institution but not a hospital! An upright stern woman she was, but our wild imaginations conjured up the shenanigans she got up to while students were away at lectures. Could have written a book back then! Breaking the rules is mandatory, if you live under a curfew. Basement dwellers came to the rescue to allow wayward students in, through the windows, after the stroke of midnight when the carriage had departed. A lot of pulling, tugging and hauling through the windows that kept intruders out, it took a lot of muscle and a certain level of stamina, while trying not to create a ruckus. I have never felt that adrenalin again, living on the side of transgression! Daredevil years they were — what with a night out on the town with a handsome beau. Those were the days. Those stolen weekday nights were fit for a queen — top dining experience. Forget fish and chips!

Life lessons crept in when political meetings began. The campus was a hotbed of political thought. Change was in the wind — the message was clear. Every student had to commit to the cause, it was *our* cause. Every voice had to add to the volume crying out for democracy. It was a commitment to reject oppression like the greats that went before. The hostel community was on call for information and dissemination of the latest on the resistance. The government had called a state of emergency — authorities prohibited large gatherings. On the campus, select eyes and ears brought the latest global reactions on the move for democracy. Dissatisfaction was growing. Conversations carried on late into the night and into the weekends at home. Everyone was in awe of the underground activities playing out. Within, the fire of resistance grew with each maturing day.

Those who opposed change had to face the consequences. Being stigmatised was ugly, nobody wanted that label when the majority cried out in hunger and pain. The arts flourished with stories, in poems, songs and dance — change was close — war dances and cries, the salute, power to the people and slogans of peace touched every tongue.

Demonstrations and a boycott of lectures, as passive resistance, created a united force against inequality. And with every story that crept in from the outside, anger and compassion burned brightly.

The law spoke. Authorities shut the campus. A passionate rising of voices that called for peace and democracy — denied with that decision...

Security forces manned the entrance and exit points enforcing the dismissal and closure of the hostel and campus at large. In an age of no mobile phones, queues lined up at residence pay phones to make a two-minute call home.

'The campus has closed. We have to leave tonight.'

All students in residence hailed from towns, cities and provinces a long way across the country. Did I tell you this was an ethnic university? Single-race, apartheid zoned, academic institutions. There was no multicultural mingling allowed, in fear perhaps this might encourage a cross over to the dark side of political thinking, or impact on flouting the *no love across the color line* law — heaven forbid the tainting of the Immorality Act! No interracial love! How is love immoral? Now that is a whole different story, a rather long story. But love finds a way.

The scramble to get off campus brought growing concerns that dreams for the future were over. Several weeks later an official letter arrived with a serious message.

You may return to campus for a peaceful resumption of lectures, for the purpose of gaining a tertiary education. Please read and sign the documents attached to this official notification.

Twenty pages followed with all the things *not allowed* or expulsion with immediate effect would apply.

THE RETURN WAS as chaotic as the departure in settling into an unsettled world. The next morning the air was sombre, eyes were averted on the long walk across to the main campus. Seven close friends met at the duckpond after the first lecture, close to the cafeteria, to take in the winter sun and grab a coffee.

What followed, was total mayhem nothing close to the shutdown.

The sound of shattering glass, somewhere near the administration block, then raised voices and the anxious thud of running feet and the chant, 'Run, run, get out!' — interspersed with what sounded like the popping of gunshots. Choking smoke clouded vision, friends lost in the skirmish to get out. Coughing and spluttering with riot police stomping behind in heavy boots, carrying batons which were used with force, knocking students to the ground as they passed. A peaceful entry was now a violent brawl, a one-sided brawl as defenceless students ran to the nearest campus exit, falling down embankments while looking back for missing mates. It was an ambush set up by the powers that be. Memory pulsated in every mind... Sharpeville... Soweto... One by one like dominoes...

The campus shut for another two weeks. Newspapers blared that students reneged on the peaceful terms of return — silent on why riot police were present, camouflaged in campus buildings and on campus grounds. *Booted with batons and teargas* — silent.

LIFE LESSON LEARNED. Truth and trust were not a given but when entwined with compassion it armed for life with an unfailing understanding that injustice based on the hue of a God-given skin was intolerable and inhumane.

Every heart and every mind lived with the glory that traversed through a dark valley to the sunlight of survival with the words of salvation firmly planted on all lips:

Mandela isu tata iAzania.

He did.

Long live freedom!

PART II

THE RAIN

One should never be ashamed to cry. Tears are rain on the dust of earth.

 —Charles Dickens

THE RAIN

The rain came down in bucket-loads, drains overflowed, scraggly, rake-thin dogs with spines protruding, sought cover behind abandoned oil barrels, truck tyres, and under rusty chairs.

It rained for fourteen days and fourteen nights, relentless, soaking rain, saturating the ground to a mushy mess, a sinking hole, keeping folks indoors, idle and restless.

The river rose, threatening to gush over to swallow the land. Thuli watched the downpour from her front stoep, hoping, praying that Vincent would be home soon. The children were hungry, the flood prevented her from going to work — the buses stopped coming into the lowlands. The local village administrators barricaded the main road pick-up and drop-off zones, they allowed no vehicles in as the river continued in an angry swell. Thuli pondered how emergency vehicles would get into the valley, visions of being air-lifted with the children troubled her.

She had half a bag of samp and mielie meal. The steamed maize combination constipated her and the children — several days of eating the same food, the only meal available, left the children crying at night, rolling around with stomach cramps. She had three young mouths to feed, the unborn child she carried was incubated from the treacherousness of the relentless downpour. Her baby was due on Christmas day.

Thuli worked as a house cleaner for the Grenville family. They owned a large bookshop in town. She received payment for the hours she worked, not a penny more, no pension fund, no sick-leave, and no maternity provisions were offered. The Grenville's cook, a kind-hearted old man, put aside a concealed bag of food for her family whenever she was at the house cleaning, ironing and washing clothes. She left the packed food intact, never eating a morsel, saving it all for her family. Once she came home with a roast chicken and vegetables. Seeing her two boys relish every bit of the meal, filled her with joy. She rubbed her protruding belly, drooling for some of that meal to still her hunger.

They were trapped with no access to fresh food, live chickens, fruit, and herbs. Disease teemed beneath the surface, stagnant water was a haven for breeding termites, as one rainy day led to another.

HER ELDEST BOY, Thabo was a skinny nine-year-old. He missed seven days of school — his school was on the other side of the swelling river.

Vincent worked in the city, a hundred kilometres away. He was a packer at a large courier company. He came home six times a year, every two months, with a supply of groceries and limited cash for his family.

Five-year-old Vusi was growing by the minute, his shoes were tight, giving him blisters and aching feet. He walked with a pigeon-toed gait, to ease his pain. In desperation, Thuli chopped off the front of his shoes to allow his growing feet to relax.

She was a proud woman, she fought her own battles, never begging nor borrowing from anyone.

Mrs Jordaan, the Grenville's neighbor, wanted the hardworking and trustworthy Thuli to work at her house too. She offered her some ironing, after her shift at the Grenville's. She looked forward to the extra cash and had already planned how she would use it — shoes for Vusi was number one on her list, then books and pencils for Thabo and a new dress for baby Gertrude.

Gertrude was born eighteen months ago with Down syndrome. Her brothers adored and protected her. Her beautiful smile and open, loving arms brought great joy to their home.

Thuli boiled a pot of water on her coal stove. The chopped wood chips were soggy, she used a dwindling bag of coal to get the stove going. She told Thabo and Vusi to drink the water as hot as they could bear, to lessen the pain of their constipation before they ate another bowl of samp and mielie meal.

'Eat more samp rather than putu tonight, boys, it will ease your tummies.'

'When is Baba coming home?' Vusi asked, 'I miss him, Mama.'

'We all do Vusi, we all do, but I cannot be certain when he will be home with this rain cutting us off.'

Thabo looked at his mother, his furrowed, concerned brow made her unhappy that her boy was forced to be older when his father was away.

'Can we go into the town to get more food, Mama, what about Gertrude, she must be in a lot of pain in her tummy too, she cries all the time.'

Thuli held back tears, going into the town was impossible with the roads closed off, and if they tried to, they would risk their lives.

'Eish, the weather does not allow us to do that, we have to pray that it stops. I can't leave you alone here.'

Thabo touched her belly.

'Mama, you need to eat too, the new baby needs food from you.'

'Oh, Thabo, you are my old man! You should not worry

about these things now. You are a good boy, a growing lad, I need to fret over you, not you over me, my son.'

'Let's have a family hug, Mama, it will make us feel better. Vusi, bring Gertrude here.' Thabo assumed the role of head of the household with ease.

He stood behind his mother, stretched out his arms, the four embraced in a hug, clinging to each other, whispering a prayer for the rain to stop, and for Vincent to return. Thuli felt emotional these days, her overactive hormones, added to her anxiety. She swallowed the urge to sob, she had a duty to keep the children happy and safe.

Persistent low, heavy clouds brought nightfall creeping in earlier than usual into the valley for that time of year, shrouding the once verdant terrain and starlit sky in an eerie blackness.

Thuli organised the children's bedtime routine before it got too dark. A pack of six candles was all she had, and not enough matches to sustain lighting them for a few more days. She fed the children a watered down putu, made them cups of insipid tea, then swabbed them down with gritty water, soiled from clogged, overflowing drains and water-pipes. After reading a few pages from an old copy of *The Wind in the Willows*, that The Grenville's had thrown out, she sang the soothing lullaby, *Thula Thu Baba* to calm her babies to the words that promised the return of their father, their Baba, by dawn.

She sat on the woven grass mat, beside them, watching them sleep — a lioness on guard over her cubs, the rain continued its plummet and water levels continued to rise.

She was seventeen when she was pregnant with Thabo, Vincent did the right thing by marrying her according to tribal custom. In the eyes of the law, tribal marriages were not recognized. If anything happened to Vincent, she had no claim to what little he owned.

Work became scarce in the little town, ten kilometres outside the valley, forcing him to look for employment in the city, after Gertrude was born. Vincent knew Thuli struggled without help, he wanted to put Gertrude in day care, and later in a school that catered to her needs.

Working as a packer on weekdays, as a security guard at a night club on Friday and Saturday nights, and at a car wash in a shopping centre on Sundays, exhausted him. His visit home this month was delayed — his family was stranded by the angry river between them.

Thuli teased him about being pregnant again, during his last visit home.

'What are the chances of a woman getting pregnant when she sees her husband, once in two months, huh?' she laughed, 'I must be very fertile, or God has a plan.'

Vincent looked at her, his eyes narrowed with suspicion, his mind ticked with his greatest fear.

'What are you trying to tell me, Thuli? Are you carrying *my* child?'

She turned around, glared at him, angered and saddened by his insensitive remark.

'How can you ask such a question? This makes me very unhappy. Dear God, this is not right! Maybe I should leave, is that what you want?'

'Do you blame me for feeling like this? You are a stunning woman, Thuli, I am not home for long spells. You must get lonely. I worry. I have little to give you and you don't complain. I have sleepless nights wondering who's trying to steal you from me.'

Her eyes were red. She was angered and touched by his insecurity.

'You need to control your thoughts, Vincent. Yes, I miss you, but I am not lonely with our beautiful children around me. I love you more than you realize, and our children mean the world to me. Please, please don't say horrible things, you are only here for two days. Life is short, you know, let's keep it happy, please, Vincent.'

'I'm sorry, I'm just a jealous guy, and who can blame me, look at you! The guys I work with, complain that their wives run around with different men while they are away working, this disturbs me, it eats at me.'

'Please don't label me like the other wives, you ought to know me better by now. How long have we been together? Have I ever given you a reason to doubt me? This jealousy will destroy us. If I wanted to be nasty, I could say you have a few city women on the side. I love you too much to do that to you. Trust, *ja*, trust is important in a marriage, you better believe it.'

Vincent could not look Thuli in the eye, aware that he had made a terrible mistake in asking an insensitive question.

'I know, I know, I must mind my tongue. I will never look at another woman, nobody can hold a candle to you. All I want is my family's comfort. I don't want you and the children to struggle through life.' He reached out to hug her, she pulled away, but her heart melted, she smiled, leaning on his arm for assurance.

'No more babies after this one Vincent, okay?'

She was teary now, remembering this conversation, she touched her belly, whispering to their unborn child, 'our youngest child, you are protected in there.'

She pondered whether Vincent spared a thought for them, had he forgotten them? He was two weeks overdue on his visit home. All telephone lines were down in the area.

Food was running low, the river level continued to rise…

IN THE CITY, Vincent was sleepless with worry, his family lived adjacent to the river. The only entrance was via the rickety bridge that ran across the river.

Daily newspapers raged with the conditions in the valley. Vincent took whatever job came his way. The extra cash was necessary to provide a home in the city for Thuli and the children, if he was to see his family every day. He was restless, not knowing how they were doing. Was their food supply running low with Thuli not being able to get to work? They depended on him bringing two month's supply of groceries — they would now be down to next to nothing.

A colleague told him about a delivery job that was paying well. All it required was dropping off a few boxes, once a week in the next town. He hesitated at first, but the money was too good to pass up. All he could think of was how the extra cash would ease the struggle for Thuli and the children. He stashed the cash in a box at the bottom of his cupboard, planning to take it home as soon as the roads were accessible for his safe return.

On the third Sunday of his delivery run, he rang the doorbell as he had done before.

The door flew open — two burly police officers grabbed him, kicking him to the ground, yelling as they handcuffed him.

'You are under arrest for illegal possession of firearms!'

'There's a mistake officer, I don't have any firearms. Please believe me!'

'What do you think you have been delivering here for three weeks? We've been following you from a tip-off we received.'

The officer opened the boxes. Tucked under layers of black fabric, covered with polystyrene chips, a dozen AK 47 rifles gleamed up at them.

'Do you mean to tell us you did not know what you were delivering? What a load of rubbish!'

Vincent was faint. His mind jarred with thoughts of Thuli and the children, starving, waiting for him.

'Sir, I didn't know, I took up the delivery job because I needed extra money for my family, we have a new baby on the way, please believe me...'

'You all say that! We are taking you down to the station for a report, and you will spend the night in a holding cell until we can figure out who is behind this illegal manufacture of these firearms!'

'No please, not a cell, not jail! I will make a report, please, I have to go to work in the morning. My children will starve if I don't work.'

'You should have thought about that before you got yourself into this pickle, hey! I don't understand you and your people!'

Vincent was shoved into a paddy wagon and flung into a cell that night.

The rainfall continued into the eighteenth day, trees collapsed, sliding onto houses, the ground now incapable of holding its roots as lashings of rain washed away loose soil. Water-logged cars, bogged in mud served no purpose, nobody could leave nor enter the valley.

Thuli's kitchen sprung another leak, she placed a large rusty oil drum under the gaping hole. She warned Thabo and Vusi to keep Gertrude away from the oil drum.

While Vincent was locked away in a cell, Thuli remained positive, unaware of his situation.

Thabo grew restless, he was her child with an old head on his shoulders.

'Mama, please give me some money, I will go to the village, the spaza shop close to my school will be open. I can bring back food supplies.'

After many days of resisting Thabo's plea to go out for more food, the rain lessened, stopping for a few hours, offering Thuli hope that Thabo could venture out.

She dressed him in a large woollen jumper, track pants, tucked his father's rain jacket around him, and gave him the cash she had.

'Even if you can get bread, butter and apples that will be enough for now, Thabo.'

She hugged him not wanting to let him go. He struggled to breathe and wriggled out of her arms.

'Promise me, if there is any danger, you will turn around and return home, okay?'

'I will, Mama, I promise, I will be back soon, you know I'm fast, just like the springbok, you won't notice I'm gone.'

She watched him leave, her heart heavy that her child had to do what his father should have been there to do. Her son with an old head on his young shoulders had responsibility thrust upon him, too soon.

His feet sank into the soft ground, slipping as he tried to speed up his pace. He turned around twice, smiled, waved, and disappeared into the early morning darkness.

Vincent's work mate visited him at the cell that evening.

'Vincent, I'm so sorry, brother, I didn't realize the work involved transporting illegal firearms, I'm really sorry. I should have asked first before I told you about the job.'

'Not as sorry as I am for not asking. My greed for the extra cash got the better of me. It's my family that concerns me, you know. I can't go to them.'

'I'm trying to see if I can raise some money to get you out of here.' He lowered his voice and added, 'these police officers like a bribe. It's not a promise, but I will try. Have you signed any documents yet?'

'No please, not bribes, please. I don't want any more problems! They asked me for a verbal statement, that's all at this stage. I need to contact my wife and have no means to do this. She has no access to any communication with the havoc the rain has caused there.'

'Give me her details, I will seek to take word to her, if possible.'

'Please don't say anything about me being locked up. She works for the Grenville Bookshop owner's family. If you can contact them, perhaps they might get a message to her, I don't know, but please try.'

Thuli dressed the children that morning after Thabo left. Vusi had a million questions about his brother's whereabouts. He stood on the stoep looking out for Thabo's return.

'Come inside, Vusi, the rain is gushing down again. Your brother will be back this afternoon.'

'But, Mama, Thabo says he is as fast as a springbok, why is he taking so long?'

'Come, let's start the stove together for some tea.'

Nightfall closed in on the valley.

Thabo did not return.

Fear crept into Thuli's heart. She consoled herself that Thabo had stayed the night because the rain returned after he left that morning. She needed to believe he would be back the next day.

Vusi was agitated and Gertrude was in her own happy space, unaware of the growing anxiety around her brother.

'Can we go out to look for him tomorrow, Mama, maybe he got hurt or he's feeling sick.'

'We shall wait and see in the morning. Go to sleep now and pray that Thabo is here when you wake up.'

Her nearest neighbor was three kilometres away, she couldn't risk going out for their help. Leaving the children alone at night was not something she would do, the thought of losing them loomed like an endless nightmare.

Thuli sat on the woven grass mat watching her children sleep, feeling the pain of the empty space where Thabo slept, next to his siblings — her boy with an old man's head.

She prayed for Thabo's safe return. She cursed herself for sending him out. The deceptive rain stopped for a few hours, tricking her into thinking Thabo would be safe and back home soon.

Vincent spent the night in an overcrowded holding cell. Men belched, cussed and threw up around him. He clung to the iron bars, afraid to move to the centre, fearful of the rumored assaults in prisons.

He was here with the worst in society, for a crime he did not commit with knowledge or intent.

At 5 am he was released with instructions not to leave town until the hearing, in two weeks.

He ran all the way to the courier warehouse, hoping to make it in time for his morning shift.

The security guard halted him at the gate, telling him he had been fired. He was under strict instruction not to allow him entry.

'I'm so sorry to be the bearer of this news. You are a good man, but when the boss speaks, it's God speaking. I hope something works out for you, brother.'

He handed over his ID tag and left with a sinking heart. He had nothing... nowhere to go, and no one to turn to. Thuli would throw him out if she knew he had spent a night in a cell and had an impending court hearing. Being role-models to the children was an unquestionable expectation. Having a father with a criminal record is not what she would support. Vincent walked around the city streets, losing all hope of ever seeing his family again.

How would he explain this to Thuli, and make her believe he was innocent?

THABO DID NOT RETURN by morning.

Thuli paced the stoep with agitated energy. The rain vented its anger in a torrential, merciless gush. The horizon was invisible, suffocating her.

She walked to the mushy water-sodden area in front of the house. The fog had descended into the valley. She stared out into the advancing cloud, waiting, hoping...

She blinked when two moving specks emerged from the fog, on the left side of the river. Her parched, fear-laden voice wanted to call out, 'Thabo!'

His name was locked in her throat as the figures bobbed towards her, one carrying something unidentifiable, the other looking at the rain-soaked path, treading with caution... she recognized Vincent's rain jacket... had they found Thabo? She wanted to run to them, fear pinned her to the ground — her heart hammered like a thousand frenzied drums.

She looked into the man's face... searching... wanting to know if they had found her boy.

All she saw was a limp, lifeless rain jacket.

'Mama,' the man said without looking at her, 'they told us to check if this is your child. He was washed up on the riverbank.'

Thuli shook her head, aware in that devastating moment that they had brought Thabo home.

The man placed her cold, wet son on the stoep where he often waited for many hours, expecting his father's return from the city.

Thabo lay dead, her nine-year-old boy with an old head on his young shoulders — gone forever.

The river he thought he knew so well, on his way to school, every day, had claimed him when the storm's wrath returned.

Her boy with dreams was no more.

Thuli's primal scream and convulsive sobs, echoed across the valley with the pain of loss that only a mother, a protective lioness, could feel for her dead young one.

A QUIET MOOD infiltrated their lives. Vusi retreated into long spells of silence, he stepped out on the stoep and stared into the horizon, hanging onto the hope that Thabo might, by the grace of God, return... someday...

Two weeks later, once the roads had cleared, and his case was heard, Vincent returned to pain and joy. He remembered how Thuli saved him from a life of hell when she fell in love with him, giving him their beautiful baby boy, Thabo. Had she not had their baby, she would never have married him — she pulled him out of his wayward ways of wasteful drinking and gambling. Their son made them a couple, then a family.

Their boy with his old head was snatched from them.

Two months later, on Christmas Eve of that fateful year, Thuli went into labour. The midwife was there to assist her with the birth. Vincent was on the stoep, waiting. Vusi and Gertrude slept on the floor next to him. It was a hot, humid, African summer night.

He looked up at the stars when he heard Thuli's agonised scream, and then the shrill musical sound of a newborn baby's cry.

He rushed to the room where Thuli lay. Their baby boy was healthy and determined to show off his vocal strength.

Vincent kissed Thuli, he stroked her head, swabbing her forehead with clean water.

She had endured much since the rain began. They had lost the joy in their lives, but it was time to rebuild.

A lone star shone a brilliant light that night. Vincent felt Thabo next to him, urging him.

'Mama needs you to be here with her, Baba, don't go back to the city without her. Please Baba.'

This time he answered.

'I will my son, I will. Rest in peace, until we meet again.'

He heard the soft soothing sounds of *Thula Thu Baba*. This timeless lullaby calmed troubled children in a land where life and death were given and taken in an instant.

Thuli gently rocked their newborn baby boy to sleep.

PENELOPE

Penelope lived on the south side of town, the daughter of Bryce Consentes, a prominent northern estate business-man. He was respected for his contributions in advancing start-up businesses for young entrepreneurs. He had the monopoly over the thriving coffee shop industry in the country.

DURING THE FESTIVE period of 1979, he held a staff dinner party at his warehouse, on the outskirts of town.

An extravagant soiree with food that could feed a starving nation, alcohol on tap, and musicians flown in from distant shores, hit the newspaper headlines as the shindig of the year. This made Bryce a demi-god in the eyes of his employees and the disadvantaged sector of the country.

ELLE, an eighteen-year-old country-bred girl, abandoned her high school education, in her final year, to join Bryce Constentes' company. She created an elaborate story, when she left home, that she was his latest recruit in starting up her own coffee shop.

While working as a cleaner at his warehouse, she clung to this dream.

Elle was a striking, tall, golden-haired young woman, with penetrating crystal-clear blue eyes. Her beauty attracted admiring glances when she was, cleaning and clearing up the warehouse or serving Bryce's guests.

He asked to see her after the party. He had some additional work to be done, and he told her she was the only one he could trust. Her excitement was uncontrollable, half hoping she was close to being granted funds to start her own business.

That night, Elle understood that a young woman should never be alone in the company of a man who had too much alcohol in his bloodstream, and power loaded on his back. Bryce Consentes forced himself on her — nine months later to the day, not a day before nor a day after, leaving no room for his denial, Penelope was born.

He let Elle work on at the warehouse until her swelling belly was difficult to conceal — he asked her to leave with the promise that he would cover all medical bills leading up to the birth of *her* baby. Bryce Consentes, the respected youth-start entrepreneur, made it clear he would give her a once-off cash *payout* after the child was born, then she was to disappear — he did not want to see nor hear from her again.

PENELOPE ARRIVED into the world on a cold, wet September morning in an exclusive private hospital, on the north side of town. Elle spent three days at the hospital and left with nowhere to go.

Consentes fulfilled his promise, a parcel with cash waited for her at reception, her once-off payment for silence.

Single and jobless, with a newborn infant to care for, and the knowledge that she would be thought a disgrace to her family, left her no option but to return to the country.

Elle boarded the train for a six-hour trek with her newborn baby in her arms.

She got off at the station and took the bus which stopped at the main road in her hometown, then walked two kilometres to her parents' home.

She had written to them saying she was taking a break and wanted to see them — she said nothing about her situation.

Her father, Tobias, was laid-off after an accident at work. Her mother was blind after a long spell of advancing glaucoma. In the last three years, she had no vision at all. The shadows she saw, were drawn like a heavy curtain, shutting her off, leaving her to readjust to a life with complete blindness. She knew her way around the house, but her husband had to take her wherever else she had to be, outside their home.

Elle felt the burden of guilt and shame. She was bringing her problem to her parents, who already struggled with life's challenges.

Her brother Fred had a scholarship to a prestigious university in America.

She walked up the steep incline to the house, her heart filled with trepidation.

This was a one-horse country town where everybody was privy to what was cooking in their neighbor's pot. Nothing was private in this small town.

Elle hated the close-knit community. The inhabitants in this rural area knew everything about her, from her school grades to her onset of puberty.

She was back with so much dirty-linen and nowhere to hide. She was thankful the infant slept in angelic peace. Elle knew fretful babies invited curious or irate attention. Baby Penelope stretched and wriggled, in need of a nappy change and feed. The nurse told her to continue putting the baby on her breast although her milk had not come. In her naivety, she puzzled over how the baby would be fed if there was no milk in her breasts, how would she quench her thirst?

She needed her mother more than ever.

Her father opened the door before she could press the doorbell.

The warm smell of roasting potatoes wafted up her nostrils. She loved her mother's crisp on the outside, melting buttery, rosemary-flavoured potatoes.

She heard her mother's voice.

'Is that Elle? Bring her to the kitchen, please Tobias, I have a hot pot of coffee and jam and cream scones waiting for her. Tobias? Are you there? Is it Elle at the door?'

Her father's silence was enough to make her want to turn tail and run the hell away from his wrath. He stood transfixed, staring at the wriggling bundle in her arms. The tips of his ears grew crimson, it spread to his cheeks and down to his neck. She saw the sweat on his brow and took a deep breath.

'Is this *your* child, Elle?' he hissed through clenched teeth.

She stared at the gleaming parquet floors, years of waxing and shining had left a brown crust along the white skirting boards. Her mother's finicky attention to detail was no longer a feature of their once pristine home.

'Yes, father, she is mine, not by choice, but she is my baby.'

'What do you mean, Elle?'

He stood like a barricaded fortress with no intention to invite her in, demanding that she answer his questions.

'Did you sleep around, for the heck of it? Is this how *I* raised you? How will *I* explain this to the neighbors, the congregation? Everyone! How?'

She continued staring at the floor, afraid to look up as he went on and on.

'Dear God, Elle, what have you done, this problem does not go away, it stays with you for the rest of your life. Did you spare a thought for that?'

'I know, father. It was not me sleeping around for the 'heck of it,' it's a long story. Are you going to let me in?'

Exhaustion and frayed nerves made her weak under her

father's glare, she needed a bath and a bed — she needed her mother's arms, and her warmth, and good food.

'Well, let's see what your mother has to say about all of this! She's unwell and this shock will kill her, you know.'

'I'm so sorry, I had no one else to turn to, please believe me. I did not... '

She heard her mother call out, 'Tobias, aren't you going to bring her in?'

Her mother stood at the kitchen entrance facing the front door.

'How many weeks is the child, Elle? Is it a boy or girl?'

Elle slumped to the floor with Penelope on her lap. She grabbed her mother's ankles and wept for all the problems she had invited to their door.

'I'm so sorry mother, so very sorry, I never wanted this to happen, I had dreams for a better life for you and father. It's a girl, mother, she's five days old.'

'Dear merciful God, you've just had her, and you've traveled out here on your own. Here, put her in my arms and freshen up, you need to eat something before you can feed this little one.'

Elle had half expected this reaction from her mother who always lived in her father's shadow. Now, she ignored his attitude and presence, she spoke from her heart for her daughter.

Elle walked to the bathroom, paused at the door to catch what her father was spitting out in lowered tones.

'Are you going to encourage her in this awful situation? How will you hold *your* head up in this district? What will Mrs Mumford say when she comes snooping around? Nobody must know about this. She must leave as soon as she's eaten something. I will not have her in the house, do you hear me?'

Her mother's determination surprised her even more, she was unaffected by her husband's insistent demand.

'She is your child, Tobias! How can you be so unfeeling? The district and all the Mumford wagging tongues can go to hell, I tell you! This is *our* family, and besides a baby cannot be concealed. She may stay if she wants. It's my responsibility to help her recover. She's weak and emotional with all she has endured.'

'I will have nothing to do with it, I'm not staying a minute more under these circumstances. I can't be under the same roof with this going on! Call me when she leaves. I'm taking the next bus into town. I will let you know where I am once I've figured out what to do!'

His selfish attitude was no different to his stern rules when she was a child.

'Tobias, don't be silly. I need your help while Elle is here with the baby. She needs to rest.'

He walked out, without a goodbye, his clothes nor a backward glance. He walked away from his wife, daughter, and whether or not he liked it, his granddaughter.

Elle stepped into the dining room when she heard the front door slam. Her mother sat rocking the baby, cooing and cradling her in her arms.

'Elle, what's baby's name?'

'Penelope.'

'My mother's name, how wonderful to hear her name again. Thank you, Elle. Everything will be all right. You wait and see. Your father will be back, I know.'

'Mum, Penelope's father is my boss. I am ashamed to say, he raped me on the night of the staff Christmas party. He paid the hospital bills and gave me some cash, but he wants me to disappear. He won't see Penelope, nor acknowledge her as his.'

Tears streamed down her mother's face.

'Oh Elle, I'm so sorry that you had such a terrible thing happen to you, I feared it when you left for the city. You have nothing to be ashamed of, he is the one who should be ashamed of himself! You should have told your father, perhaps he would have stayed. What a horrid man, your boss turned out to be. I should expose him. The world thinks he's wonderful.'

'No mother, I wish to erase this memory and focus on raising

Penelope who did not ask to be born, her story is sad enough without me adding more scandal to it by exposing her father and making her identity public.'

'At least report it to the police, he has to give you child support.'

'I prefer to never be indebted to him! The rest of my life must be planned for, before I can even consider these issues. Right now, I'm at a complete loss on what to do.'

'Yes, you have many things to think about. It's more important to look after yourself and Penelope now. Have you had a medical check-up for yourself after the birth?'

'I had good care at the private hospital but I'm still bleeding after the birth, is that normal?'

'A little is normal, but not for too many days. Let me know if it continues.'

'Will you keep Penelope, Elle?' her mother whispered, afraid to ask such a question.

'I am determined to do so. Every girl needs her mother. I will be Penelope's mother, just as you are to me.'

'Praise you, sweet child, I have little to give you, but my love and support are always for you. I hope you know life will not be easy without a job, as a single parent.

Her mother stopped talking as she continued to stroke the baby's head, more words were unnecessary now. They had already said too much.

'Thank you, mother, your love, and support are all I need. I am sorry that father left because of me.'

Later that night baby Penelope developed fever, Elle's milk had not come — her breasts were hot and inflamed.

Her mother rang Dr Manet who agreed to call at the house. Elle and Fred were delivered by him, all those years ago. He listened to all that she told him.

Dr Manet administered a few drops of paracetamol to bring Penelope's fever down. He left a feeding bottle and recommended giving the baby warm water during the night, and powdered baby's milk in the morning.

Elle neglected to tell him her breasts were swollen and painful. Getting Penelope settled was all that mattered to her.

The next morning Elle set out early to the local village to buy powdered baby's milk. She felt faint but pushed on. Her mother told her a new family to the area was running the general store. She was relieved that a level of anonymity was possible.

Penelope was fretful that morning, crying for long stretches until she exhausted herself. Elle's mother heard a knock on the door and assumed Tobias was back.

Mrs Mumford stood at the gate, hands on her hips and a curious look in her eye, peering over Elle's mother's shoulder. She said she overheard a baby crying the night before and early that morning.

Elle's mother could not conceal the baby's presence in her home, but she could protect her daughter from being the subject of village gossip.

'Elle is visiting us with a sick friend's newborn baby, she is helping care for the child while her friend recovers.'

'Dearie me, she came all this way for *you* to help her with the baby?'

'Yes, she needed my help.'

Elle returned with the baby's milk, greeted Mrs Mumford and rushed past her to the bedroom, aware that her eyes lingered on her swollen waistline. Her mother excused herself and shut the door, leaving the curious neighbor no opportunity to come in.

'What did she want, mother?'

'She heard Penelope crying and came over with her usual curiosity. Let's bath the baby and get food down her. How's your milk, any sign of it appearing? It might dry up now that we're putting Penelope on a bottle.'

'Not yet, mother.'

She did not say a word on the difficulty she had when raising her arms or that the pain in her breasts had increased.

Penelope had a strong set of lungs, Elle knew her mother was right, it was impossible to conceal a newborn baby from the ears and eyes of a meddlesome neighborhood. Women like Mrs Mumford sniffed around, bored with their little lives.

The next night, Elle came to her mother's room. A storm was raging, lightning flashed, plunging the house into total darkness.

Elle was sick, she was burning with fever, her breasts were aflame, she was dizzy, her mother swabbed her down, but it was too late, within an hour Elle slumped over next to her, her pulse was faint.

Septicaemia set in, she left the situation untreated, her declining immune system, and high stress levels escalated the condition. Elle's mother was distressed, she had no contact details for Tobias. Although the electricity was out, the phone line was active. In her panicked state, all she could remember was Fred's telephone number. He called the doctor. Dr Manet arrived in the early hours of the morning. Soaked to the skin on his walk from the car to the house, he apologised for trailing water into the hallway and advised Elle's mother to step with care.

All signs indicated that Elle had died an hour ago, soon after she slumped over onto her mother.

Three days later, Fred arrived from America, he located his father in the city and brought him home.

They buried Elle in unrelenting rain, in a private ceremony. Her mother, Tobias, and Fred were the only people at her funeral.

Her mother wanted her to be laid to rest beside her grandmother, her newborn baby's namesake. Little Penelope lay in a stroller, sheltered from the pouring rain, zipped in from the harsh weather.

The family drove home, lost and distant, each staring out the car window, watching the soft, set to stay rain, falling with unyielding momentum.

Tobias, with his stone-age values, was adamant that they should return Penelope to her father, Bryce Consentes. Fred left for his college exam the day after the funeral.

Tobias located Penelope's reluctant father — he had her put out for adoption through an agency. Both father and grandfather denied any filial connection to a beautiful baby girl, leaving her with an uncertain future.

Loss and pain in her life without Elle became an eternal graveyard, deep in her mother's soul.

She never recovered from her husband's callous attitude and actions. She died eighteen months later, still not on speaking terms with her husband — her broken heart was unfixable at the thought of Elle's untimely passing, and Tobias's refusal to care for Penelope.

Fred remained in America, blaming his father for his sister's and mother's deaths.

EIGHTEEN YEARS LATER, a bitter Tobias who had lived out his hermit days, after his wife's death, never going out, except once a year, to the gravesites of his wife and daughter, placing flowers at their headstones, then shuffling with a funereal pace back to his empty house.

A letter arrived one morning to shake his desolate world.

Dearest Grandpapa,

You may not know me, but you know of me. My name is Penelope. I am your granddaughter, Elle's child.

My wish is to pay homage to my mother, on my eighteenth birthday, and I seek permission from you to visit her gravesite. I want to meet you in the hope you will accompany me to my mother's grave. I would like to talk to you about my mother, to understand who she was. She died before she had time to experience life, just a year older than I am now. I am desperate for a connection, a link, whatever you can offer to give me a memory of my beloved mother. Only you can share her life with me. Please let me know if you will do this for me.

I intend coming over in a fortnight. I'm including my telephone number in the hope I hear from you.

Love, Penelope.

His heart leapt with joy and sank with anxiety in the same instant. What if she resented him for disowning her mother? What if she…?

He spent every hour contemplating all the 'what ifs.' They played over and over in his head. How would he explain his actions to Penelope when he could not answer to himself why he behaved the way he did?

He placed all the childhood photographs he could find, first birthday, holidays, school photos, on the dining room table, in readiness for Penelope's visit.

TOBIAS SHUFFLED to the front door on that sunny September morning.

'Hello Grandpapa, it's lovely to finally meet you.'

She kissed him on both cheeks, hugged him and laughed like a little girl.

Overcome with emotion he had not felt for many years, his heart thawed, melted, and glowed. He stepped back, surveyed Penelope from head to toe.

'Dear God, you look just like your mother. Come in child, I've missed you,' he whispered.

GHOST TOWN

A small town with a population of six hundred lay nestled in the valley at the bottom of a large, majestic mountain — hidden and forgotten.

Nobody visited the town, it was a quick dash-past, not a stopover for tourists, driving to major cities with its rush of distractions.

Boredom set in for young people, a small library with vintage books and a movie theatre that repeatedly played old classics was the sum of their entertainment.

Danny, Patsy, and Lance were a close trio since childhood. They created their own sense of excitement during their weekends together. Danny bought his first car, a second-hand Fiat 128, with the money he saved from his casual job at the library. Saturday nights brought adventure during their driving jaunts around the little town.

They set off, one evening, for a night drive up the mountain, something none of them had done before.

As children, their parents cautioned them to keep away from the dangerous mountain. They asked no questions — the mountain sat in forbidding silence, a majestic mystery.

During the summer months, it gave off a lavender hue,

during winter it lay shrouded in a blanket of fog, until noon. The left side had weathered away to appear like a child's face with bulbous cheeks, two crevices for deep-set eyes, a chubby chin and pixie craggy tips for ears. Patsy and Danny often surmised whether the rock face was that of a girl or a boy.

'Hey Danny, I hope your car is in good nick, it's a long, steep drive up there at this hour.' Lance said.

'Yeah, it is as good as it can be for this model and year, I suppose. I wish I could afford a new car. My dad used to say, one day he would get a van 'out of the box.' I never knew what he meant and imagined a car literally in a box until mum told me it meant a brand-new machine, like a present in a gift box, unused.' The three of them laughed as they recalled the phrases their parents uttered which fed a wild imagination.

'Thanks for inviting me on this ride, guys,' Patsy said, 'I appreciate being included, you both are the only ones who are so nice to me.'

'Hey Patsy, if anybody is bothering you, spill the beans, Lance and I will put them in *their box* for sure!'

'You're funny Dan! I don't cry over those nasties anymore — life is too short for that.'

The car chugged up the steep mountain pass, the track narrowed as a layer of fog crept down like they had never seen before, on a summer evening. It appeared as a large bale of linen winding its way towards them.

'Turn on the music, it feels creepy with that fog rolling down. How did it appear so suddenly?'

'Don't worry Patsy, it's quite safe, the heat of the day and moist cool air up here must have caused this.'

The radio crackled, spluttered and died.

'The reception is poor up here. Do you have a CD we could play?'

'Check the glove box, I'm not sure what's in there.'

Danny tried turning the radio on again, he pressed the power button, rolled the dial around a few times, trying to pick up a station. The crackling grew louder, then it stopped briefly until a faint voice made them gasp.

'Good evening folks…'

'What the hell was that?' Patsy whispered, 'it sounded so real!'

'That was a woman's voice, it must be from some station Danny caught while rolling the dial,' Lance reassured.

'It was like hearing someone on the telephone.'

The experience spooked Patsy. Danny and Lance remained calm.

The incline was steeper at this point, the vehicle groaned, stuttering to a slower pace.

'How much longer before we reach the top?' Patsy was impatient, wanting to get out the car.

She was a restless child, always edgy, riddled with the uncanniest fears, and obsessive about doing everything in 'threes' — three rapid sips of soft drink, then a break before the next set of sips, she would scoop food in three small helpings onto her spoon, chew rapidly, rest and continue this way, repetitively scooping three times, chewing, resting and starting again. Patsy locked doors and windows even when she was visiting Danny in his family home. People avoided her, finding her behavior odd, some found it offensive seeing her eat the way she did. Danny was the only person, as her older cousin, who stood by her like a brother.

Both did not have siblings. He understood the loneliness of being an only child and the need for inclusivity. At nineteen and twenty-one years old they clung to each other for support.

Danny lived with his mother, promising her he would never leave her after they found his father hanging in their garden shed, five years ago. He left them with no closure, no reasons, just walked away, taking his pain with him. Danny was almost sixteen when this tragedy struck his family. He took on casual jobs after school to help his mother pay the bills. She slipped into depression, not saying much to him since the suicide.

Lance was adopted by an elderly couple after his biological parents were killed in a car crash in the South of Spain, no family stepped forward to take responsibility for his care.

He arrived in the town when he was ten, after being a ward of the state for two years. His adoptive parents were close friends with Danny's family. Lance's friendship with Danny and Patsy made them more siblings than friends.

Danny tried several times to get the radio going, there were no CDs' in his glove box.

The fog gradually lifted as pummelling hail deafened them.

'Oh nooooo!' Danny wailed, 'where did that come from? My car will be flattened!'

After five unending minutes, the hail stopped, rain fell like silver needles, sparkling each time the point landed on the windscreen. Then a steady downpour followed.

Patsy shivered, pulling her jacket across her chest, zipping it up to her neck.

The vehicle grunted, spluttered, and came to a grinding halt.

'Have we broken down Danny, what are we going to do?' Patsy asked.

The engine was dead, all three sat stunned when the dashboard lit up and the radio crackled. The woman's voice they thought they heard earlier was distinct.

'Good evening folks, have you come up to help me, I'm desperate, please don't run off and leave me. I need help.'

The sound of the woman's voice was that of an older woman. Her hesitation and soft tone suggested she was afraid.

At this point, Lance lost his usual equanimity.

'Danny, are you pulling a stunt here? If you are, I will never speak to you again!'

'That's ridiculous Lance! I'm just as petrified as you! Why would I do that?'

'You've been dabbling in some strange things these past two weeks, what with that awful Ouija board you're been getting us to play!'

'What the hell? That was a bit of fun, I don't know what this is?'

Patsy trembled, her eyes were shut, her lips mumbled something incomprehensible as she rocked back and forth.

A knocking sound on the passenger door made Lance dive into the driver's seat, pushing Danny up against the door.

He refused to open the door.

'Open that door, it might be an injured animal!' Danny yelled.

'No way! How are we going to help anything when we are stranded here?'

Danny reached over, pulled out the torch from the glove box and shone it into the inky darkness. All three shrieked!

A thin, pale-faced, spiky-haired woman, looked at them, her wide staring eyes, searching, pleading...

Danny froze, the torch rigid in his hand, casting a beam of light across the woman's face — she looked like a relic from an ancient, forgotten land. Her grey-white, mould-covered cheeks, hollow eyes and sparse hair sent shivers down their spines. The apparition placed her powdery palms on the window, her gnarled, curved tendril nails, blackened with dirt. She began jimmying the door, forcing it to open. She pressed her face against the window, staring over Lance's head, craning her neck to get a look at Patsy.

Danny flicked off the torch. They were silent, mesmerised by the cascading sound of falling rain.

THE SUN STREAMED through the car window at 5:30 am the next morning.

Danny started the engine. The radio came on with the familiar voice of a popular male presenter whose humor they enjoyed. His tone was far from light-hearted that morning. He warned listeners not to venture out of town — more rain was approaching and predicted to last for many days. He cautioned that flood warnings might be issued.

'We must have fallen asleep. We better get going before that rain arrives again, and these roads lock us off from getting home.'

Patsy pointed to the window, not speaking. She was pale and disoriented.

'What's wrong with you Patsy, you look like you've seen a ghost?' Lance said.

'Where's… wwwheee… where's the lady?'

'What lady? You must have had a dream.' Danny nodded in agreement with Lance.

FROM THAT DAY on Patsy never spoke another word, she refused to leave the house. Danny visited her, read books to her, all she did was stare into the distance, pointing to something he could not see.

The unspoken legend of this town was that a woman went in search of her missing child, a little girl, almost fifty years ago. The girl disappeared in the woods, during a school camping trip, on the lower terrain of the mountain.

They were never seen again.

DIVIDED SKY

On a humid summer evening, late in December, children in the apartment building played in the wet courtyard downstairs. An afternoon thunderstorm kept them trapped indoors. Portia stood on the upstairs balcony watching them play as she listened to the churning drainpipes in their rainy-day gargling ritual.

A mournful wailing from a woman penetrated through the choking sounds of filthy rain-filled drains. The woman ran into the adjoining apartment block.

'Somebody! Help! Please help! Abe's been stabbed! Please, someone, please!' She was hoarse from the strained volume of her wailing.

Portia stood rigid, watching Abe's wife, on her knees covered in blood with no sign of Abe in sight. A few neighbors rushed across to the kneeling woman, her children tried to aid her to her feet. She flopped like a rag doll.

Two burly men from an upstairs apartment carried Abe into the building, water dripped off his left shoe, the other foot was bare. His shirt was ripped off at the sleeve, and blood mixed with rain trickled down his once white shirt.

They placed him beside his wife. She wailed louder and

louder, her escalating grief, gripped by fear for her future without Abe.

'My husband is dead! What am I going to do? Abe, wake up, please wake up!'

Tears streamed down Portia's face and fear chilled her heart as parents rushed their children indoors. Abe's children's mournful wails echoed through the corridors, drowning out the sounds of youngsters playing and the stuttering of clogged drainpipes. That humid December evening set the tone for change in a close-knit downtown suburb.

An anxious, unsettling night crept in.

Police and ambulance sirens, an orchestra out of tune, played amidst the grief-stricken wails — Abe was whisked away. Women stood around, frowning, afraid, whispering in lowered tones. Men hovered shaking their heads in disbelief. Portia's mother went over to the woman to help her into her apartment, the door shut behind them.

Portia's cousin, Veronica, appeared from the street in front of the building.

'Uncle Abe was stabbed by a group of fellows, they robbed him of his wages. When he resisted, they poked him in the neck, got his jugular.'

'How do you know all this, Veron?' Portia begged.

'Well, dad was speaking to uncle Noah outside the building, I listened in, or else no one will tell us anything. I overheard them say some black fellows killed him. Adults think we should be seen and not heard! I am nineteen and need to be told things, you know.'

'No, that can't be true, theft happens because poor people do not have jobs and money to feed their families — don't say, black fellows, please Veron! It could have been anyone.'

Portia panicked that racial tension was brewing in her happy neighborhood.

'What a load of rubbish, you watch too many of those political films that your father feeds to the family, we are all going to go like uncle Abe one day, you wait and see.' The venom in Veronica's words was the first ripple of fear that infiltrated the small apartment community.

Portia held her hands over her ears, she did not want to hear any of it. The sound of the blocked, filthy drains was better than hearing her cousin display such deplorable views.

'I don't believe it, stop scaring me, I love Mama Agnes — she will never harm us. She washes my hair and plays hopscotch with me.'

'Nah! Not Agnes and her family, the black thugs on the street will finish us off. They hate it when their people work for our families.'

Veronica had many opinions, she felt she knew the way of the world. She wore the racist views of others like a second skin. She was kind and generous, always bringing little gifts for her cousin on payday. Veronica enjoyed chatting to Portia, often confiding in her about the prospective suitors her father was arranging for her. She had a boyfriend. He was studying for his law degree — her father would not have a bar of it. He would only promise her hand to the highest bidder.

Upon her twentieth birthday, the year he deemed her marriageable, he would barter her like a bag of perishables, for something more, treating her like a worthless thing, discarded as someone else's problem.

Veronica's personal unhappiness shaped her prejudiced thinking.

PORTIA WAS a decoy for Veronica's love tryst with her dashing boyfriend. During such encounters, the girls would walk together to the store, next to their apartment block, under the pretext of buying a tub of face cream she needed. Rainy days were the best to allow an unnoticed escape, for a few stolen kisses.

There was something raw and romantic about kissing in the rain, snuggling up against each other.

Portia waited under the bus shelter nearby, while Veronica disappeared down a side alleyway with her lover. She found herself daydreaming of meeting such a handsome young man some day and enjoying stolen moments in the rain.

She watched a small crowd of people pass, some walking hand in hand, others rushing, afraid the rain would ruin bouffant hairstyles, and women carrying heavy bags of groceries. Her imagination would take her on a journey through the lives of those walking by. She wrote little stories in her head about each one.

Phoebe Gumede carried her laden parcels up a steep flight of stairs. Her family would wait for her, eager to savour the treats she brought back. Delicious Chelsea buns, coconut snowballs, and fresh cream doughnuts. Phoebe worked from 4 am to 11 am at the bakery on North Street. She showered and went off to her second job at the clothing factory downtown. She was the sole breadwinner, she wanted her children to have a good education, to make a difference for themselves and others. Her husband was a waste of a man, sitting around all day drinking beer and playing cards.

She would continue creating little scenarios of those she thought might have interesting or difficult lives. After Veronica's stolen kisses, for that week, they walked home in silence. Portia was tight-lipped, telling no one about her beloved cousin's clandestine meetings.

She knew if she ever spoke of Veronica's secret love affair, her future would be sealed, far sooner, with a walrus suitor that her father would whip up to save himself from disgrace. He was a proud man for whom family name and a healthy bank balance took precedence over his daughter's needs.

Abe's murder was on the minds of all, including the children of both apartment buildings. All surmised about what led to uncle Abe's untimely death. The culture was such that older people were referred to as 'uncle' and 'aunty' even though they were not blood relatives. Downtown apartment society considered this a non-negotiable mark of respect.

Portia remembered the boy from number eight referring to Mr Kimmy as 'Tom' and not 'uncle Tom.' The next day he was black and blue from the belting his father gave him. Minding one's manners was significant in those days.

After the murder, children were prohibited from going to the shops without their parents, outdoor games had to end before sunset. Mothers were vigilant, shouting out their children's names to *get inside before your father comes home from work, otherwise, you're gonna get a belting, you hear me!*

Fear engulfed all.

Women would knock on each other's front doors when their husbands took a deviation on the way home on payday. If their husbands stopped off at the pub, their fun would come to a grinding halt when a posse of local men would hunt them down and drag them back to their anxious wives and children.

Everybody knew everybody's business. All the women would huddle together whispering.

'What do you think of Jessie's husband? He did not return for five hours after work. Poor Jessie she was losing her mind with worry, I don't blame her after what happened to poor Abe.'

Grapevine gossip was on the lips of the idle and afraid.

Husbands had entitled respect from their wives who never referred to them by name, it was always 'Jessie's husband, 'or 'Rita's and Robyn's father.' If Jessie referred to her husband to others, she too would say, 'Rita's and Robyn's father.'

They considered it bad luck, an unexplained omen, to utter one's husband's first name. Such was the value system of the people of 'Indian origin' or 'Asian' race, and at one time referred to as 'Plurals', depending on the government's preference of racial labeling.

Portia hated this side of apartment living. Everyone knew

what she had for dinner, everyone knew what her school grades were, everyone knew if she helped her mother tidy the house or not, everyone knew if she received mail, everyone knew if she had been grounded by her parents, or lo and behold, if she got a belting that night. Everyone knew the girl from number fourteen went to the movies with the boy from across the street, Mrs Adams never failed to pass on the word.

'My Cheryl told me she saw them going into Grand Theatre, holding hands, can you believe it? What disgraceful girls! Thank god my Cheryl is a good girl.'

Portia kept Veronica's secret woven around her heart. Nobody would speak about her in this nasty way, least of all, loudmouth Mrs Adams, whose name she refused to tag with, 'aunty.'

Abe's death was fodder for all parents with daughters. They would put girls on a curfew. Thanks to Mrs Adams' tell-tale, loose-tongued, trouble-making mouth — the curfews were tightened!

Everybody knew everybody.

Apartment city was a swing-door of personal stories made public.

The general dealer on the main street greeted the apartment children, and those from surrounding cottages with his usual curiosity.

'How are your parents? Busy? How's school?'

The small store, packed to the rafters with washing powder, toilet rolls, milk, bread, eggs, soft drinks, chocolates and every sweet delight that would have a child wearing dentures before they got to high school, was the hub of the district.

After school delights made the store a popular haunt. When children did not have the extra pocket-money required for a favourite sweet-treat, which was often, the storekeeper would come to the rescue. He was a shrewd businessman who never let a dime slip.

'Pay me the balance tomorrow, okay?' followed by, 'don't

forget now, or no sweets ever again. You don't want me to tell your parents you come here every day after school.'

The threat was enough to make children who did not pay their sweet-treat debts on time, cough up the next day, even if it meant, begging, borrowing or stealing a few coins from unsuspecting parents.

A close-knit community involved everybody in each other's cultural or religious festivals. During the holy month of Ramadan, the children did not come out to play. The corridor lights timed the end of the day long fast as a cue to sing in unison, *lights are on, lights are on,* relishing the thought of a treat in the offing.

Excitement for the time of day after the long fast had ended for their friends, was a shared culture and history.

Before breaking the fast, the most irresistible aroma of exotic food wafted across to the next apartment block, saffron, sweet yellow rice, biriyani spices, and ghee, enveloped the air like a magic carpet gliding in from distant shores. All waited with anticipation for the invitation to savor a delectable treat. Every year the neighborhood children were invited with grace and generosity to the breaking of the fast meal.

A wonderful community that looked out for each other is how Portia saw her downtown suburb. The other apartment blocks that came up, years later, brought a strangeness to the society of houses and apartments that once felt the joy, pain and loss of each other. Death is something she faced early in her young life, seeing countless neighbors lose loved ones from ill-health, old age and other strange circumstances.

While people were close and protective of each other in apartment city, value for life was cheap in the dark days of apartheid where fear and gloom lurked.

Portia's family engaged Agnes, a loyal and hardworking woman of senior years, as their domestic employee. She traveled every day from the outskirts of town, to clean and wash and look after Portia when her mother returned to work.

Agnes sang while she worked, she treated Portia as her own child, her English was flawless. Her mother was fluent in Zulu. Portia listened with amazement to the conversations her mother shared with Agnes.

When Agnes grew too ill to continue working, she sent her daughter, Nomusa, to help run the home. Nomusa was immaculate, dressed in a black skirt and a pressed, white or pale-yellow cotton shirt. She had the unmistakable smell of *Super Rose,* a skin whitening chemical. This gave Nomusa's face a reddish hue. It was the baptism liquid of all young African woman who felt their blackness like a festering ulcer, in a country where the law glorified white above black.

Some Indian women packed turmeric masks on their faces in the hope of a fair complexion. Apartheid created the unholy belief that dark skin was the curse of shame. Companies exploited this need to be 'white,' by manufacturing a range of bleaching creams — uneven pigment discoloration became the bane of existence in pursuit of a much desired, 'fairer complexion'.

Finding a wife of 'fair complexion' was highly prized in a country where color defined every facet of life.

Women gathered around in idle chatter, fascinated by people like them, who were a paler shade of dark.

'Did you see her new daughter-in-law, white as the driven snow, I tell you. Must be mixed-blood in her family, you know.' Mrs. Adams never failed to offer her two cents worth.

Portia hated this divisive gossip, secluding herself from social gatherings that droned on with such idiocy.

She loved listening to Nomusa sing her church hymns as she bathed before she left for her home. Her voice wafted from behind the bathroom door, in soaring angelic, high, and deep tones as the beautiful light and shade in her voice. Portia listened, with her ear pressed up against the door, wanting to learn the lines, hoping Nomusa would continue for as long as she could. Nomusa, like her mother, had a compassionate and easy-going nature.

When Agnes's health failed, Portia's father decided that the family should visit her in her home, a place so close, yet so far under a divided sky. It was a stormy day, summer thunderstorms either lingered or were destructively brief. The car could only travel to a certain point up the mountain, then the upward foot trek in mud, slush, and rain — a memory her family spoke off in many conversations over the years.

Curious neighbors stepped out to behold this strange sight, a man, a woman, and a child, all 'Indian,' 'Asian' or perhaps of 'Plural' descent (depending on the government's desired label). Broad smiles lit up the arduous, winding, wet walk, uphill, to Agnes's home.

It was then that Portia's parents knew Agnes was a respected member of her community. She was an elder.

At the summit stood the little hut. Her father, a tall man, had to stoop at the doorway to enter the dark front room.

Agnes lay in a corner, wasted away, the size of a child, barely able to speak. Portia was teary seeing her this way, she looked on afraid and helpless. Agnes was a grandmother to her, seeing to all her needs.

Portia cowered when a sudden wailing erupted from an adjoining room, why was someone wailing? Agnes held onto her hand, sensing her fear. The peaceful look on her face was enough to suggest she was overjoyed they were with her.

They set blankets, mielie-meal, bread, and steri-milk down beside Agnes's bed. Chilled air seeped into the hut as they joined her family in quiet prayer.

Portia and her parents left an hour later. On the downward trek to the car, the walkway was lined with people again, singing, chanting, clapping and dancing. It was a royal send-off, something they had never experienced before.

The neighborhood came out to offer thanks on Agnes's behalf.

This was Portia's early experience of how apartheid divided society in compartments of racial inequity. The undeniable, enduring beauty within the human soul was palpable, here in the mountainous terrain on the outskirts of a small town where humility was unaffected by injustice.

THE VISIT to a plush 'white's only' suburb, to the home of her mother's white colleague, was the first trip across the color-bar for young Portia. It filled her mind with visions of white male, uniformed police officers bashing black men.

Her mother embraced the journey across the color-bar with natural ease. Portia was nervous. She was quiet, lost in thought on the drive there, observing the shabbiness of the area she lived in, filth-lined streets, crowded spaces, and then like a panning camera — an awakening from a dream — across the freeway into the plush suburb, the streets were wider, cleaner, pruned hedges, gardens in centre aisles, with well-kept plants and little shrubs, the houses were bigger, rolling park-like front lawns, beautifully laid out. People, white people, with dogs on leashes were out for a Saturday afternoon stroll.

Their car, an obscure dent in this perfect landscape, slid along in silence. Every Saturday afternoon stroller's gaze became a glare, hard eyes followed their vehicle — their dark faces peered through the window as they drove through forbidden territory, triggering suspicion they were up to no good.

Portia was dressed in her Sunday best, a yellow, crimplene dress with pearl buttons and a frilled collar. She was awkward and afraid. Her head throbbed, *we will get caught, we will be thrown into a paddy wagon — no one will find us.* Visions of the paddy wagon and men being dragged and kicked into the vehicles disturbed her walk to school each day. She saw much cruelty in her young life.

A long driveway and equally long and large front garden

made the home they were visiting seem austere. Her stomach churned a million times.

A smiling woman stood at the door of this enormous house. Her pale-brown hair and porcelain-white skin shone in the afternoon sun that draped her front entrance.

'Hello everyone, lovely to see you again and this, I presume, this is young Portia, welcome, welkom. Come in, kom binne. I love your beautiful dress, darling.'

Portia was silent, unsure of what to say when her mother prodded her from behind.

'Say thank you, Portia, remember your manners.'

Portia was unsure how she should address this friendly white woman. She referred to all who were adults as 'aunty' or 'uncle'. How was she to refer to this white woman, without offending her?

'Thank you… er … Ma'am,' is all she could mumble under her breath, she called her teachers 'Ma'am' so this felt the right thing to do.

'Aren't you just gorgeous Portia, I can be your Tannie today, do you like that?' Her voice was lyrical and kind.

Portia smiled back with a whispered, 'yes.'

The lounge room was large with a huge space between the chairs, her mother sat on the edge of her seat, eager, ensuring she did not miss a word their kind hostess uttered. Her father sat with his hands on his legs, and a blissful, serene smile on his face as he watched and listened to the warm, friendly conversation between two women of different race, under a divided sky.

The lilting sounds of a piano wafted into the room. This sent Portia off on an imaginative flight. She thought there might be a daughter playing this beautiful tune in her bedroom, or in a special area in their home. The house was large enough to have a music hall, she dreamed…

This idea was soon dismissed when Tannie stood up saying the music was too loud and walked with irritation across to the stereo to turn down the volume.

The dining room table was adorned with a beautiful crisp, white, lace tablecloth beneath white teacups, decorated with red roses, and a gold-rimmed edge — perfection on a little teacup ready for a banquet. Red and blue tiered cake-stands cradled the most delectable scones and tiny bottled jams, a dozen or more mini pastries and custard tarts filled two large silver platters.

This was Portia's first of many sophisticated high teas. She had high tea at home with her mother's beautifully baked scones and cup-cakes, but this symphony of color and design made her feel she was a princess in a palace dining hall.

Tannie disappeared much to Portia's relief, she could breathe without feeling she was on show, or that she should watch her manners. It allowed her time for a closer look at the laden table. It felt like Christmas.

Tannie returned and all four settled down to tea. Portia was quiet, declining any of the sweet treats offered, fearful that the paddy wagon would get her if she dropped the cream or jam on the crisp, white, lacy tablecloth!

Tannie insisted, 'Come now Portia, you must try something, I baked them especially for you, my liefling,' she cooed.

Her mother looked across at her, 'What would you like, darling?' Portia loved being called, 'darling,' the term of endearment made her warm and cosy.

She cooed back, 'I'll have a scone, please mummy, with butter only.'

The cream and jam teased her gastronomic juices, but she knew she could not trust her awkward little hands to guide the scone, decked with creamy delights, into her gob without making a mess! Images of flashing lights, police officers, and the dreaded paddy wagon kept her away from anything moist that had a dropping, messy possibility!

This child of apartheid, born on the wrong side of the racial tracks was out of her depth in Tannie's home.

While the adult conversation continued, Portia wondered

whether Tannie had a husband and family. She pondered how Tannie lived alone in such a big house, with no husband or child.

A pleasant self-restrained afternoon passed. Soon it was time to leave. Portia was the first one at the door, eager, ready to run out.

Her mother smiled, 'Thank Tannie for a lovely tea and wait in the verandah, we'll be out in a minute.'

Portia whispered, 'Thank you very much, Tannie.'

Tannie squealed with delight, 'Oh you dearest child, you say it so sweetly, thank you for visiting with mummy and daddy. Promise you will come again, hey.'

Portia's first visit to a home on the white side of town was a pleasant one, touched with an awkward awareness of her difference. Her father was no longer quiet on the drive home, he hissed out his discontent at apartheid injustice.

'You see! Look at these fancy homes, big properties and I tell you, they pay low land rates compared to us, who earn below the bread-line wages! Don't get me wrong, this Tannie is one of a kind, inviting us the way she did, but this country treats us like we are nothing! Like dogs! We must not forget who we are, you hear that Portia, never, ever forget!'

The rest of the drive home was silent as thunder rolled in the distance, announcing the arrival of an African thunderstorm.

The gutters overflowed, the rain pelted down from a divided sky that separated a nation, based on their skin tone, alone.

CRUEL-KIND HEART

Every conceivable spot on the floor, tabletops and lounge chairs, laden with paintings, books, ornaments, candlesticks, vases, jewellery boxes, bicycles and more — a decade of cobwebbed clutter. His obsession for collecting things didn't bring meaning to his cold world, just abundance, vacuous, cold abundance, the more he had, the more he craved.

Rainy late afternoons and nights turned a switch in his brain. It made him edgy and angry as memories of days gone by, returned to haunt him.

It rained that year, the week before Christmas, for seven continuous days. He was ten years old, he lived, breathed and dreamed, imagining he would get the toy truck he saw in the shop window on the high street. He pointed it out to his mother, she dragged him away, not a word said, no promise made.

He hoped. He daydreamed.

The rain continued into the week of Christmas. As the day grew closer... no tree... no gifts... no frenzied shopping... no invitations received, nor sent for the usual friendly gatherings, at this time of year.

Silence.

His father left in October of that year, two days before his tenth birthday. His mother took to her bed, crying, not eating, locked away.

No birthday cake, no gift.

Loneliness.

His mother surfaced after two weeks, a spectre, pale and ragged, living in her dressing gown and slippers. She smoked an endless string of cigarettes.

She never ceased loving him, she tousled his hair each time he walked past her. He ached to hear her voice again, she quit reading to him and never spoke to him again.

Silence.

He woke up early on Christmas morning, no tree, no gifts, no scrumptious lunch cooking — no truck.

No Christmas — ever again.

She died on his thirtieth birthday.

No celebration — no tears.

Christmas on the eve of his fortieth birthday, caught him unprepared.

HE WATCHED THE ELDERLY COUPLES' comings and goings for the better part of that year. They lived alone, nobody visited. They shopped on a Wednesday, went to the movies on the last Thursday of the month. Both went to the beach every Sunday morning, stopping off for a two-hour lunch at the bistro on Second Street. The old man was much slower, he shuffled, never looking up. Her arm always hooked in his. The wife was energetic, quick in step and smiled each time she said something to his silent presence.

For many Thursdays that year, while they were at the movies, he peered through their lounge windows. A mid-size, table-top Venice De Milo stood on the hallway table. A painting by Picasso, *Woman Reading*, had pride of place on the wall above the bookshelves that traveled all the way, stretching across to a plush, red, velvet-cushioned window seat — the shelf continued to the next wall, beyond the window seat up to the end of the lounge room wall. He craned his neck for a better look, a brown fluffy cat lay still, curled on the window seat.

A rich red and gold mat sat in the centre of the lounge floor. The room had a regal, untouched appearance, everything was in its museum spot. Two weeks before Christmas, a tall tree appeared in the hallway, sparkling with gold and red baubles. Under the tree, an array of gift-wrapped boxes, waited... he lingered, wanting to go in... it was too soon.

He waited for the promised weather forecast, rainfall was due, just before Christmas, they said. He double-checked newspapers for confirmation that the deluge was coming soon.

On Christmas Eve, in his fortieth year, a torrential downpour sent last minute shoppers scuttling for cover.

His brain switched — his intention was clear with the regularity of ten past Christmas eves.

He donned his black gym tights, black sweatshirt, black hoodie, strapped his black bag on his back, and slouched unnoticed into the night. The streets were quiet, not a walker nor a car. An empty bus made its solitary journey through empty streets.

A perfect night!

He sprinted as he got closer to the house. He peered in at the window.

The cosy sight before him, made his heart leap with joy. The couple sat in front of the telly, watching a live broadcast of Christmas Carols. He enjoyed seeing the old woman tapping the arm of her chair, swaying as she sang along. She poured gin and tonic into two frosty Christmas glasses. A plate of shortbread biscuits sat on a tray garnished with the holly she bought at the florist that afternoon.

He rang the doorbell.

The old woman, engrossed in her musical night, did not hear the doorbell. The television blared at high volume. Neither of them reacted.

He walked to the side of the house. The dining room sliding door was ajar. He slipped in.

As he loaded his bag with the Venice De Milo, and a few books, he looked up at the painting and decided he would return another day to collect it. He had to have it. His eye caught the title of a book his mother had read to him, he lingered, sat on his haunches and paged through the pictures in the book.

The old woman felt a cool breeze, she rose to shut the dining room sliding door. The hair at the back of her neck stiffened, she turned, shrieked when she saw him and ran back to her husband, shaking his arm, pointing to the man at the bookshelf. Her husband sat in his chair, not registering, not moving.

'What are you doing looking through my bookshelf?'

Her voice was soft. She felt no fear seeing him mesmerised by the children's book, oblivious to her voice, paging through, stopping on some pages with glee written across his face.

'Who are you, how did you get into our home?' she raised her voice, over the carol singers.

He jumped up, spun on his heel and lunged at her, reaching to place his hand over her mouth.

She bit into his hand with all her might, the brown cat, suddenly alive, jumped at him, scratching him on the face, sending him reeling across the floor.

Her husband, alerted by the scuffling, growling and hissing sounds, looked up from his daze. He stood up on unsteady feet, clutching the armchair as he rose. He lifted the silver candlestick off the coffee table and lost his balance, he fell over with a thud, his glasses flew off his face, and landed under the dining room table.

'Take all you want, just don't hurt us. Take everything, it is Christmas after all, take it!' she cried.

He looked at her, unsure how to react.

'I won't call the police, you can have the book too if you like it, is there anything else you want?'

He stared at her with his eyes wide open. She looked at her

helpless husband on the ground. The intruder rose to his feet and walked over to him, keeping his eyes fixed on her.

'Don't hurt him, please, he's harmless please, please...' She sobbed, walking towards him.

The cat lunged at him again, he shook it off with a force that sent it flying against the lounge room wall, yowling as it landed with a weighty thud.

He helped the elderly man to his feet, put him back in his seat, placed his glasses on his nose, and his gin and tonic in his hand. The old man sat helpless, accepting the drink with trembling hands, fear emblazoned in his eyes.

She stared at him, not sure what to expect next.

'Would you like a gin and tonic and a biscuit?' she asked in a gentle voice. She saw the sadness of a helpless, lost child.

He looked at her, nodded and sat on the floor next to her husband. Slowly, very slowly he stood up and put out his hand to shake hers.

'I'm sorry, I'm sorry.'

She spoke to him about all that had happened in his life. He left that night without his black bag. He pulled off his hoodie and ran like a madman let loose in the rain. It was around midnight when he got home. He took off his black gym pants and saturated sweatshirt, placed them in the outside garbage bin, showered and went to bed. For the first time, in over a decade, he slept like a baby.

The next morning, Christmas morning, in his fortieth year, he rose at 7 am, picked up a dozen white, fluffy bread rolls from the bakery on the corner of his street — the hot bread rolls that adorned his mother's Christmas table in happier times, ready for a decadent, butter-filled, crusty bite.

He walked with a light spring in his step, smiling, looking up at the shaft of sunlight, peeping through clouds, eager to greet the day.

He rang the doorbell.

The old woman's rosy cheeks and smile welcomed him. The

aroma of a warm kitchen greeted him with the unmistakable, familiar smell of rosemary lamb roast roasting in the oven.

He closed his eyes and inhaled in remembrance of his lost childhood.

She held out her arm, 'Come in son.'

WINDING FOOTPATH

A lonely, one-bedroom cottage, overlooking a beautiful gleaming white stretch of beach with red and brown speckled seashells pebbling the seashore was a writer's haven. A long, narrow, sandy walkway led to the little strip of paradise below. Seagulls knew her well, gathering around her on her morning walk, fluttering, squabbling and competing for her attention.

Five years of blissful solitude brought her the healing she needed.

She cycled to the grocery store and greengrocer, once a week, and made a fortnightly stop at the post office to pick up her mail or to send off her manuscript to her editor in the city. That was the extent of her human interactions ever since her arrival in this little hamlet.

Zeus, her Golden Retriever was her constant companion, running beside her when she cycled to purchase supplies, bounding alongside her, during her morning sprint across the pristine strip of beach. He hated the seagull interruption, barking and growling to shoo them away.

Five years before this period of blissful solitude was not

entirely forgotten, it remained hidden somewhere in the deep crevices of her psyche. The memory of love and pain lingered.

Eirene Dubois arrived at her beachside cottage five years ago, aged forty-five at the zenith of her stellar career as a psychotherapist for the City Central Police Department. She worked part-time, teaching at the university, a short walk away from her plush six-bedroom mansion. She was an Olympic Gold Medallist, a gymnast in her day. She continued the discipline of physical fitness with her own home-styled gym and morning jog. Her slight frame and height belied her strength.

She had everything life could offer — but not someone to love and cherish her.

Her four close friends had drifted apart over the years, married with children, two moved to New York to support their husbands' advancement in their careers.

Eirene locked herself in the world of work, dealing with remorseless criminals — rapists and murderers.

She had the ability to turn tough, ruthless men into sniveling, confessional children, they trusted her, felt safe she would do the best for them if they were open and truthful in what they divulged to her.

One particularly disturbing case that stretched and tested her mettle, was that of a young man, Eric Thanatos, in his early twenties, in the final year of his university studies. In a moment of unexplained madness, he gunned down his parents and sisters before giving himself up to police, accepting total blame for his callous actions.

He had no previous history of violence nor any drug addictions. He used his father's hunting rifle to kill the only family he had. Eirene tried to unlock the reason behind this brutal killing. He was a remorseful young man with a strong death wish, his self-inflicted punishment for his incomprehensible crime.

She took him into her trust, persuading him to accept that death was a defeatist way out, that he should give back to his community by educating troubled youth. Instinct told her he could rehabilitate, to transition his return to normal civilian life.

The only relative that surfaced to support him was an uncle, Daniel Mendacious, his mother's brother, estranged from the family for many years. He lived in South America and returned when he heard his sister was murdered by her only son.

The courts were close to placing Eric on parole, believing he was remorseful for his actions. Tests confirmed that he was not at risk of a chemical imbalance as the trigger for his anger and aggression.

Daniel Mendacious visited Eric during his days of incarceration, working closely with Eirene to unravel family history and any threads that could explain what happened on the night of the killings.

It started off with the occasional coffee to discuss matters pertaining to Eric, then there were dinners, then a weekend or two away, until Daniel moved in with her. He was all she could have hoped for in a partner, suave, well-spoken, educated, a good conversationalist, and attentive.

She spent most of her childhood in exclusive boarding schools while her parents ran a lucrative legal practice. She had everything a girl could desire, except love and attention that all children craved. They were remote parents, visiting her on fleeting occasions, even when she was on a break from school — they were always on the hop either on holiday or on a business venture.

Daniel was a godsend. He filled the void that had spanned many decades in her life.

She was not alone now.

Two brilliant years of companionship — not for a second did she imagine that anything could change that.

Eric had three months inside before authorities signed his parole, he could not leave town and would have to report to his local police station as part of the expected parole conditions. Eirene planned a homecoming party, searching for his old university friends who wanted to keep in touch with him. He would live with her until he found a place of his own. This influenced his parole application.

She was at her busiest at work when Daniel pressurised her into taking a long weekend away in the mountains. The reason he offered was that once Eric was out of prison, it would be a while before they could have time to themselves. Daniel loved hiking. For her, the sea held greater appeal, it ignited her soul, rested her like nothing else she knew.

There's something about a woman conceding to anything, once she has given her heart to love She saw the pleading joy in his beautiful brown eyes and melted.

They left at the crack of dawn and arrived at the mountains at dusk. Daniel picked up the cabin keys from the kiosk manager. They drove up to the love-nest, hidden among pine trees.

This was an idyllic getaway for a couple deeply in love and needing time away from the hectic and stressful demands of life. Daniel made her promise to make it a 'no work' weekend. She carried two novels to fill the hours while he went hiking.

There was a chill in the unused cabin, they lit a fire, put on a pot of tea, Eirene's beverage of choice that night. They chatted before retiring for the night.

Daniel needed to be fresh and alert for his early morning hike. He told her to sleep-in to recover from her strenuous week.

She welcomed the sleep-in and had not heard him leave that morning.

Eirene woke to the gentle pitter-patter of raindrops on the fern and palm fronds that clung to the cabin bedroom window. She jumped up, the clock on the wall was dead — her mobile phone indicated it was eleven o'clock. Never before had she slept-in this late.

She made a cup of coffee and stepped out onto the front balcony to look out at the rain that had now become a steady downpour.

Eirene pondered whether Daniel had taken his jacket as she inhaled the fresh, rain-soaked smell of soil. She listened to the splish-splash on the leaves, realising the soothing effect it had on her — something she had never acknowledged before. Nature, dressed in a vibrant green cloak, exuded harmony and freshness as a wondrous sight. She reflected on the possibility that she could come to love their mountain treks.

Daniel was due to return around noon. Eirene hurried about preparing a barbecue lunch for him, she grabbed the bags of skewered garlic prawns and marinated chops from the fridge and quickly chopped up a green salad. She started a low fire and settled down with a book expecting Daniel to arrive at any moment.

Half an hour later, she heard the squishing sound of disturbed water puddles on the front balcony.

She called out.

'Leave those shoes outside Daniel, they must be muddy and smelly!' she laughed, looking up, anticipating that Daniel would come in through the door.

She felt an arm grab her from behind.

'Daniel, you rogue,' she giggled, 'you snuck in through the back, cheeky devil!'

His grip tightened around her neck — she saw his image cast in the window in front of her. The figure clutching her throat was tall, hooded, and masked.

She coughed, choking.

'Why are you doing this? Are you teasing me, or do you mean to hurt me?' she gasped.

He was silent.

Her feet were bare, she was still in her pyjamas. The fire poke was on the floor in front of her. She stretched her legs, using her gymnast toe flexibility to grab the metal poke. She lifted the bottom half of her torso with all the strength she could muster and flung them over her head — the poke got him square in the left eye.

He screamed, falling with a thud. She ran to the kitchen, grabbed the meat cleaver, and danced around him, threatening to use it if he attacked her again. He jumped at her with one hand over his bleeding eye. Now she was unsure if her attacker was Daniel, behind the mask, under the hoodie.

Eirene hesitated… he stretched his arm out to grab her throat again. She lunged at him, chopping the air until she gained an advantage when his impaired left eye, obscured her from view. She struck him on the neck. Blood spouted in rivulets down his chest.

She grabbed her van keys off the coffee table, ran out into the rain, jumped into the vehicle — her foot slipped on the accelerator, tyres skidded. She took off at high speed. The kiosk was closed. She drove to the filling station, down the road — it was deserted.

A pay phone stood at the fence, to the right of the building, she grabbed a few coins from the centre tray, and ran as fast as she could, slipping and falling over several times. She got through to 911.

'A police car is on the way. Stay where you are.'

Ten minutes later an officer peered at her through the van window.

'Are you sure it was your partner who attacked you? Please confirm if his name is Daniel Mendacious.'

'I left without looking behind the mask, or under the hoodie… I'm not certain that it was Daniel but the perfume the intruder wore, smelt like the one I gave him for Christmas.'

Two police officers escorted her back to the cabin.

A large blood stain had oozed onto the lounge, centre rug. Bloodied footprints led to the front door.

Nobody was in the cabin.

Her fear made her a ragged, agitated mess, unable to work as a psychoanalyst. She sold the house, moved to this hamlet, her little slice of heaven — she had left Eric and Daniel behind for her new lifestyle, away from the shadows.

Five years later she had written a bestselling memoir of her life, a shadow of her former self as an acclaimed therapist. She was a victim of her own mind. Two more books followed, gaining recognition for her creative ability. She enjoyed the anonymity of writing under the pen name, 'Elpis Athena' — she refused all speaking engagements, podcasts and television interviews, she valued her solitude, more than ever, it gave her peace and space to give voice to the stories she wanted to write.

Zeus remained her faithful companion, she loved her cosy cottage with its winding, sandy footpath, leading from her front door to the shore. Life was blissful.

Rain prevented her early morning jog that day. She developed an ear infection that left her exhausted after three consecutive sleepless nights. She stood on the verandah, sipping her coffee with Zeus curled at her feet, she looked out at the downpour as it covered and closed the crisp, blue horizon of the sea.

Eirene blinked.

Coming up the winding, saturated, sandy footpath was at first, an indistinguishable figure, head askew, flopping to one side.

The gait was unmistakable!

She stood fixed to the spot.

Her mind screamed.

Daniel!

TOBY

S talks hung thin and limp, lowered with each searing day. Brittle, sparse and ready to snap, dehydrated by the ferocity of the summer.

Water restrictions were in place, dams were at an all-time low this early in the season. Remote farmlands faced a lack of sufficient water for human consumption.

Kisaan was at his wits end, five sheep lost during the last week and his wheat crops continued to wither. His two boys and pregnant wife could not remain at the farmhouse. He knew they had to relocate to his in-law's home until the situation improved. He had to stay on to protect the property, livestock and what remained of his arid crops.

Finances dwindled and banks refused to assist struggling farmers — summer heat eroded human compassion. Kisaan had to let staff go with no funds to pay their wages. Razumihin, his loyal assistant stayed on to assist him, grateful for a roof over his head, and a bed.

Burning, merciless heat, the sun's penetrating glare, high above them, raging on, venting its anger against the earth.

The rain was nowhere in sight.

The once, lush rolling fields, and the golden glow of wheat were now brown, black, and cracked.

Kisaan's wife and children were preparing to leave, quibbling over whether they should take Toby the family dog with them.

He was a majestic Labrador, lean, sleek and fearless. Every night, he slept at the children's bedroom door. He was alert, attentive and had a sensitivity that made him human. He ate meals with the family, enjoying the same food. The heat was slowing him down.

On the eve of Kisaan's family's departure, a violent storm erupted, unannounced. Lightning strikes hit the ground in quick succession, threatening to set the crops alight.

Wide, rectangular sheets of rain gushed down. Soon gutters were overflowing fountains. Razumihin could not contain his joy, he ran out into the rain, dancing in a frenzy, his large gold earring dangling on his left ear sparkled in the rain. The children watched him from the lounge window, laughing at his crazy dance, mimicking him.

A voluminous sound of thunder rolled for an unusual length of time, then two successive bolts of lightning struck the ground, one sent Razumihin hurtling in an unending convulsive twitch. His body writhed on the soaking earth. His hair was aflame as the rain continued its avalanche. The children stared, mute, wide-eyed.

With no warning, the bedroom wall collapsed, sending Kisaan's wife running into the lounge. The floor shook with volcanic force, moving, sliding. The children clung to each other. Their mother reached out to grab them when a wall of water shoved her and the boys out — the house collapsed behind them.

The water rushed, gushing forward, tossing and turning them, their mother was nowhere to be seen. Kisaan was in the barn, moving the chickens to higher ground. The barn was solid enough to withstand the force of the rain.

The house floated on a sea of water, with the children hanging on to the rafters.

Toby stood at the highest point of the floating structure, shaking himself off after the soaking he got from being submerged below the house. He howled, a primal hyena wail, summoning the moon to calm the storm.

The rain poured down, then stopped.

Calm, still air commanded the aftermath, as debris floated along a muddy slush — chairs, beds, and tables were washed down a stream that appeared after an hour of steady rain.

Kisaan's wife had passed out, she lay under the rubble of her once beautiful home — now floating in muddied waters. The children clung to the wreck, their eyes searching for their mother.

Heavy black clouds loomed overhead threatening to erupt again.

Toby's howl echoed through the silence. His raised head and elongated jaw released a sound none of them had heard before.

The mangled mess, loosened by sinking soil, tossed and turned like a shipwreck on turbulent seas.

A tiny ray of sunshine appeared through splitting clouds.

Toby stopped his wailing for a second, then started up again, long wails from low to high, on and on.

The water slowed down — the frenzied thrusting of the house now a gentle bobbing mass. The clouds continued to part, sending sunlight down to the ravaged earth. Tree tops passed as their home continued to journey down the newly formed wide river.

Kisaan's wife opened her eyes, with the sun streaking over her. She tried to raise herself from under a large wooden plank. She craned her neck for a glimpse of the children, she called out to them. The youngest pushed forward to get to her, he fell over with a sob. She told him to stay where he was.

They hung on for over an hour. Toby's wailing subsided, he

stood at the edge of the collapsed structure like a captain on watch.

Helicopters were heard in the distance. Three came into view. Toby wailed again, upping his volume, hell-bent on being heard and seen. He stood on a precarious plank, to add height for his visibility.

A blue rubber dingy floated in. Three men wearing yellow life jackets and Kisaan in a red jacket waved like a windmill in blustery winds, wanting his family to see him.

He stood up shouting at the top of his lungs to let them know he was alive and there to take them to safety.

The children shouted out and waved back, letting their father see and hear the joy they felt upon seeing him. Emergency services got to Kisaan before he was washed away by the force of the water. He was hanging onto a tree top when they found him. The barn's solid foundation kept it upright, but the rising water submerged it during the height of the storm.

Toby's howling was now a broken whimper akin to that of an exhausted child, relieved to see a parent.

The treacherous operation of lifting the family onto the helicopters to safety was the next hurdle.

The air rescue team rolled down a harness.

'We have to get you out of here as soon as possible. Another storm is approaching. Hook the harness to the belt around your waist, and we will pull you up. Lift yourself up to give us a hold, use your body weight. Don't look down. It's safe. We are here.'

Toby grabbed the harness as the rescue team dropped it, running to each of the children, pushing their hands onto the rope to get the rescue cracking. He gripped the harness between his teeth, prostrating to give the children a lift, to allow them to be pulled up with ease. After ten, terrifying minutes, suspended mid-air over their floating home, they were pulled into the safety of the helicopter.

Toby shoveled the debris around Kisaan's wife, digging in his snout with manic speed, trying to loosen the plank and other pieces that trapped her. Kisaan saw her struggle, the weight of the wood weakened her legs. He did a daring jump onto the floating house, and gently lifted her, and hooked her to the harness sending her up to safety.

'Please hurry, we are under instruction that the storm is advancing this way again.'

The rescue crew urged Kisaan to hook himself to the harness. He pushed Toby forward.

Toby stood rigid, planting his paws to the ground, in an unmovable cemented grip.

'Hurry sir, we have no time to waste, get hooked to the harness ASAP, the dog can follow, after you.'

Kisaan looked at Toby, urging him to come closer, he hooked himself and up he went — the house, a reluctant sinking ship, disappeared.

Toby was gone.

The children and their mother sobbed.

With a sudden eruption of laughter through his tears, the youngest boy pointed ahead, animated, glued to the window.

There was Toby, swimming the marathon of his life, trying to keep up with the helicopter that held the children.

The rescue crew threw him a rope. He struggled to grab it, slipping back into the water. Then he did an almighty jump, grabbed the rope between his teeth and coiled his body around it. They yanked him to safety before he lost his grip again. Without a harnessed hook, he was at risk of falling back into the water.

The children cheered, clapped and laughed when Toby landed with an awkward slide, and rolled over inside the helicopter. He rushed to them, licking them like they needed another drenching.

The house was gone... the sheep... crops and faithful, trusted, hardworking Razumihin... gone forever.

Kisaan raised his hands to the clearing skies, giving thanks to the heavens that they still had each other.

RAINING SOUL

She arrived in winter rain, hopeful and ready to embrace a new life. Seven days of rain seemed like a normal occurrence. She never imagined the rain was there to stay.

IT WAS the summer of any December in her chosen homeland, everything looked promising, on the precipice of a new year. Things were unfolding, a new job that had chosen her, the warm glow of the memory of being invited in, looking past her 'blackness,' lingered, found no fault, and welcomed her.

What more could she ask for? Euphoria over the job secured, and a much-needed visit to the Motherland or Die Vaderland, depending on where she stood in the racial and social stratosphere was a promised post-Christmas gift.

Perfect!

Everything glowed on the horizon of life. A lightness of step, the ultra-white smile, and noticeable perpetual diamond sparkle in her eye made it a magical precursor to the destined year to come. Frantic journaling, scribbled to record and capture the unfolding bliss, at that moment, and all moments, as the hopeful predictions on more that would unfold, hovered like a brilliant light.

Hope reigned.

Arrival in the Motherland was hot, sticky and busy, people shouting, baggage handlers wanting to escort her to a taxi, for a small fee, or perhaps all her possessions. Years of absence did much to change the psyche of reaction, upon her return.

The cherished Motherland was now an estranged step-mother, her alienated child forgotten.

Amidst the fanfare of family reunions, and food galore, the holiday season passed in a haze of endless dinner invitations. The animated chatter centred on the promise of the New Year. Overwhelming family love made up for the initial strangeness, a newcomer, in a former homeland.

She was relieved to be back in her chosen migrant-homeland, but it was tinged with nervousness for all that was yet to be realized. She questioned, was it a dream, and did she have the right to a better life?

She walked on a cloud, ever since the acknowledgement — that they wanted her, infused her with a sense that she was worth the gamble, needed after all. They looked past her skin tone, ethnicity, and neutral accent.

Preparations began — clothes, a flash handbag, perfume, and how can one forget, the much-needed fashionable pair of shoes for the position.

The day dawned, a full week, orienting to the new situation, the long drive, jet-lag, introductions, and questions.

'Where are you from?'

'Where do you live?'

Was there a faint grimace, lingering for a moment then passing like a permanent shadow?

'How many years have you been in the game?'

'Do you have children?'

And then…

'I hope you won't regret your decision.'

'Be careful…'

What happened? … Everybody was smiling or was that just the website?

One must look beyond the so-called pleasantries, to 'fit in,' 'assimilate' to forget where you came from, afraid of the words, *go home, go back to your country.*

Such is the life of the eternal immigrant, expecting so much, looking so different — the difference — yes, only skin deep, just the upper epidermis. A thicker skin she had not grown, cherishing and hoping for a life altering experience.

The rain set in, no sunshine in sight, in this, the Promised Land.

Each encounter never failed to highlight her difference. Shopping in a suburb close to her home, seeking relaxing retail therapy. Dreaming! Hopes dashed on that post festive season day. Wonderful retail browsing turned into a soul-destroying nightmare.

Security guard
Body search, bag search
Outside the store
But the goods were paid for?
Horror! Horror! Horror!
Step aside!
Up against the wall!
What is this?
Why?
Pardon me.
I get it!
Black skin
How dare you browse?
And shop at leisure?
Ulterior motive
Anger
Anger
No stolen goods found

No apology
Picking up scattered
Personal possessions
Injured personal pride
Reputation destroyed
Crying
Trying to retrieve
Her dignity
People staring
People staring
Dear God
What must they think?
Letter of complaint
Anger
Then
Airport, airport?
Fear! Fear!
Checked the bags
A hundred times
Palpitating heart
Sombre faces
Step aside!
Random drug check
Random bomb check
Step aside!
Cleared through customs
Why another bag check?
Fear
Fear
Butterflies
Honest, upstanding citizen
Why her?
And not a million others?
Is it because…?
Why?

Sorry
Sorry
Not our staff
Shopping centre staff
We did not train that trash
Sorry
How about
A two-hundred-dollar
Voucher
For the trouble caused
To shop
At our store
How dare you?
Dignity and
Self-respect
Cannot be bought!
You've taken it
It was hers
She was born with it
You stole it!

THE PERSISTENT, pervasive questions, *where do you come from, do you speak English at home, she is quite exceptional, considering… what language do you speak?*

Her passport
States she's naturalised
Who are you to ask?
Badger
Badger
Haughty noses
Sidelong glances
You look like a hippy today
Jeans and tee-shirt
Hippy?

Looking
Searching
Trying
To label
Find fault
Head down
Work hard
Make your mark
Work hard
Work hard
You will be rewarded
How?
When?
The rain set in
Forcing departure

The rain crawled into her soul, stealing her laughter, drenching her joy. She retreated to bed, slept, woke, went back to bed. It was a dark, bitter, cold, wet world, she could no longer face.

She had miles to go... What brought this rain, she did not expect, not here... Was she to blame for being silent and kind? Was she to blame for not speaking up, did she leave it too long?

It ate into her soul, a storm that comes on a blissful African summer afternoon.

It rained for many years — each rainy season bleaker than the one before.

Dreams of home returned, a mono-cultural world. How dare one dream of a multicultural world, free of eternal black rain? She had no right!

Stay in your box
Safe
Keep your psyche intact, don't let it rain upon your soul.

Such were the longings, dreams and visions etched in a journal, untouched, searching for new endeavours, living in eternal hope, for the stroke of an ink-filled pen, casting wondrous words, immortalized in time, a living memory, a quest for a paradise on earth, a paradise left behind, for the hope of fertile rain, a new life.

She struggled along
Hopping from
Place to place
Levels of rain varied
Good weather assured
In some destinations
She worked hard
Very hard
It is the way
The only way
Her people know
Work hard
Say nothing
Go unnoticed
Yet he…
He noticed her
Watching waiting
Coming closer
Elbows touching
Eyes undressing
Awkward
Uncomfortable
Eyes searching
Words shaming
Leave her alone
Half-blood
Full-blood
She's human
She's woman
Let her keep
Her dignity
Can't you see?

Don't you know?

You've destroyed her

Day after dark day, as night becomes bright day, she finds her space, her own space, out of the rain, into the glorious sun of life.

Alive in solitude, doing what the calling brought, the drying of black rain.

She is here, the rain has stopped, in solitude she must remain.

She can be heard whispering, across a summer breeze, beside a lake, along a seashore.

She is here.

This is home.

DESERT QUEST

A trek across the desert had left them silent and detached. Forty days on arid sands, burning days and chilly nights, sandstorms and no sign of rain, tested their bond.

Harsh, isolated solitude pervaded their lost togetherness.

They traveled, not losing hope, searching for the footprints of their ancestors.

Nothing remained without a sense of personal history or a connection to extended family biography.

Growing up American had given them a life they would never trade — a good education, friends, an abundant lifestyle, and a glorious childhood.

Ura and Uri, born seven minutes apart, were inseparable and devoted to each other. At thirty-five, some admired their bond, others found it strange, and some thought it perverse. The people who loved them celebrated the closeness they shared.

Their parents married and migrated to America as young scientists seeking new shores. Their personal hardships propelled the decision to take this leap of faith, for their future children.

Uri and Ura were born three years later, a beautiful baby girl and a handsome lad, to an ecstatic couple.

Living isolated lives, their parents knew no one else other than the people they worked with. They were the universe to each other, letting no one else in, apart from their children's friends who were welcome guests in their home. Uri and Ura were raised American — their parents were obsessive about not enforcing culture and language upon them, allowing them to grow in their own soil.

No extended family visited — no evidence of other family existed. With no ancestry, they remained rootless.

Uri and Ura had a wide social circle, their father referred to them as Miss and Mr United Nations. They laughed and chatted, enjoying the kaleidoscope that made up their children's mateship. Friends came and went as they chose, staying over, turning up at odd hours.

Uri's and Ura's father, Adam, was the eternal student — extending and expanding the frontiers of his scientific capabilities. He shared deep, meaningful conversations with his children's college peers.

Ura was much like his father, with a bottomless desire for knowledge. As an archaeologist, he bore a wise, older air. Uri was a geologist. Earthquakes and volcanoes were her passion. Her fascination with these destructive natural forces, led her to New Zealand, Bali, Japan, Indonesia, and the Philippines.

Earth's mysteries set her curiosity on fire.

The deaths of both their parents, while holidaying in Sri Lanka, during the devastating tsunami, left them scarred, shattered, but determined to live the legacy their parents created for them.

They were proudly American, yet the ancestral tug was alive, forcing them to the desert, to feel the pulse of their nomadic ancestry.

The long trek made them sombre, silent and morose. Here they felt the blight of seasonal collisions, hot and cold within hours in one day. They took many photographs of the landscape, thirsty to capture moments of this unknown place, the home of their ancestors, as proof of this sojourn for posterity — determined their future children would know their heritage.

Kilometres of sand and stretches of green vegetation were the yin and yang of the desert, much like the relationship their mother and father shared — different personalities, in perfect harmony. Such thoughts filled their contemplative hours of grief and solitude after the death of their beloved parents.

They had enough supplies to carry them through. Their father's small battery-operated stove brought a little luxury, hot canned food and cups of black tea sustained and hydrated them.

They trekked on, day after day, not sure what they were looking for, needing to feel a connection to a past life, walking in unknown ancestral footprints.

Uri developed a fever which lingered for three days. Ura swabbed her brow and feet, gently, saying nothing, both lost, locked in their private worlds. Exhaustion? Isolation? Grief? No reasons, just a quiet acceptance of each other's grieving space.

Uri's fever slowed them down, she needed time to rest, while her temperature burned, struggling with the compounding heat of the desert. On the third night, the first drops of rain came. Brother and sister looked at each other, hope was alive in their eyes again.

They trudged through the cooler night, allowing gentle, welcome rain to caress their tired, cracked skin and parched lips.

A campfire ahead, was a welcome sight. Ura instinctively grabbed Uri's hand, cautioning her, to slow down, pause, and stop.

She ignored his pleading grip, marching on, forcing her brother to follow.

As they got closer, they saw the faces of a man and a woman, glowing in the blaze of firelight. They were huddled together, warming their hands.

The man stood up, unafraid, smiling, beckoning them to join him.

The taut, leathery weathered face of his wife, dehydrated by harsh desert conditions, peered up at them. He was stocky, strong — his eyes struck Uri as kind, yet the black ring around his light-brown eyes made him glow like a brilliant, watchful tiger.

Uri explained they were siblings trekking across the desert in search of their parents' origins.

'Who is your family?' the man asked.

Uri said all they knew was their last name. Their father had spoken of his nomadic life as a child of the desert.

The conversation continued on their lives in the United States. Throughout this interaction the woman was silent, listening, looking at each face, studying them with curious interest. They explained that their parents made a trip back to the desert, the year before they were born.

Drip by drip, like the gentle pitter-patter of raindrops, one thread at a time, untangled. Uri felt her heart quicken when the man asked if Adam's middle name was 'Bataar.' Ura grabbed his sister's hand, looking at the man with wild expectation.

'Yes, how do you know?'

The man explained that he knew nobody named 'Adam,' he saw a distinct resemblance in them to a man known to him as 'Bataar,' their eyes, he said, were 'Bataar's' eyes, the same shape, coloring and curious twinkle. He said Bataar left the desert to study, to become a scientist. That was the last he heard of him. He had no knowledge that Bataar went to America.

He glanced at his wife asking her if she remembered Bataar. Her eyes lit up, she stared at Uri, pointing at her with wide-eyed surprise, and then with narrowed eyes that crinkled to tight slits, she clapped her hands and laughed.

'Sarnai, Sarnai,' she said in a soft voice.

Uri looked at her with surprise, her mother's passport was

the only document with the name, 'Sarnai.' They knew her as 'Sara.'

The man asked them to spend the night in their ger, to keep dry, to wait for the rain to subside. He said Bataar had a cousin, he could take them to him in the morning.

They came out to the desert with no expectations. By chance they stumbled upon the man and his wife. They knew the man would reveal more if they stayed the night, now that a missing link had emerged. They were close to finding the connection they yearned.

The glowing exhilaration of that possibility coursed through their veins.

The woman continued to stare at Uri, she mumbled, 'Sarnai' a few more times, shaking her head and smiling up at Uri.

ROMANTIC RECREATION

P oetry filled their world of poverty and prejudice. They retreated to a space where inclusion was self-governed.

They belonged in the pages of novels, free of judgement, and dwindling confidence. Delighted librarians stowed away precious books, waiting for them, ready for their enlivened conversations.

School days were not the usual run-of-the-mill, girlish days, for May and June. They chewed apples and sat under the large oak tree at the furthest end of the oval, immersed in the poems that excited them and spoke to them of freedom in faraway lands, here injustice was beyond their control. High school girl-talk held no interest for them. The human spirit was their first love. Friday afternoon dances and the latest boy-crush bored them.

The Romantic era floated on the wings of poetry — the era unlocked their pain as their proclaimed birth-right, leading to lengthy conversations on life, with each poetic reading bringing a new wave of thought. Wordsworth, Coleridge, Shelley, Keats, and Blake filled their heads and hearts, keeping them safe in a sublime, visionary cloud. The evocative power of language, a single word or image softened the reality of their harsh world where girls were seen and not heard.

Post high school brought untold freedom as university life led them to deeper literary realms — they remained isolated from the social, partying scene. They saved every nickel and dime from their part-time jobs at the local library, for a trip to England, to walk in the footsteps of their Romantic literary heroes.

THEY ARRIVED in London on a dreary, wet, Saturday morning, and drove to the Cotswolds in a dreamy fog. The rolling, lush hills, and small picturesque villages transported them across time and space.

The rain created a melancholic mood — this was their self-proclaimed holy grail, treading sacred literary ground — never did they imagine during their childhood days, that such an opportunity was possible. Now they were just two hours away from walking through the pages of what was etched on their lips and inscribed on their hearts.

They arrived at the Lake District, armed with journals and sharpened pencils — this was their home for a week of blissful touring, writing, dreaming, immersing themselves in their creative passion.

Hedonistic yet tranquil. Excessive yet soulful.

The Wordsworth Walking Tour and the private Daffodils Tour had them rejoicing, remembering and chanting lines from the poem, 'The Daffodils' as they pranced in wind and rain, attracting dubious glances. Wordsworth's poems were the mainstay, the bread and butter that got them through the ruthlessness of childhood.

Without funds to buy the novels and poetry books they loved back in their school days — they crafted their own publications, handwriting their favourite verses, pressing flowers and leaves onto pages to mark their celebration of nature. May and June carried their handwritten poems to England, on this, their pilgrimage, seeking blessings from their Romantic mentors who eased the pain of childhood with endless pleasure-filled hours.

Foreign by birth, they were Anglophile at heart. England was the place in all they read.

In the Cotswolds and Lake District, each blade of grass, every leaf on a tree, every thatched-roof cottage emerged from their imagination before their very eyes. They wrote, and audio-recorded their euphoric moments, capturing all that opiate detachment could never conjure.

They had no intention of staying in London, that was for another visit to take in all they could over many days. This was the hallmark trip of their lives, one that would become a permanent, proud memory.

The Prelude, bible of their formative years was the platform on which they crafted their work, in unison with the seasons. *Book 1, Childhood and School Time* bore lines that reverberated with the dreams they cherished. Nature was their guide and eternal Mother.

Rainfall brought reclusive, creative energy to May. She composed her poems in the garden shed, listening to the gentle sound of soaking rain, enthralled by the diamond sparkles of water droplets blinking on blades of grass and glistening on deep green leaves — giant teardrops before the orgasm of a thunderstorm heightened her exaltation of nature. She wrote without restraint, a vibrant emotional being, writing in secret, under cover of protective isolation, venting her forbidden voice. If she was not seen, she would be heard.

The rain held the melody of her soul.

June crafted her best compositions when sunlight infused her space, filling her work with the beauty of nature, she relished the quietening of her eye and harmony of inner tranquility. She danced in glowing sunlit rays when golden beams poked through her windowpane, teasing her, melting her fear, growing, blossoming and setting her voice on fire.

May, prone to bronchial bouts, and spates of moodiness was confined to her bed for a week or two in the winter months. This didn't deter her from writing.

June was strong all year through, laughter and mirth ever present. She brought joyous sunshine to May's world.

They forged ahead, propping up each other against the storms of life, both becoming professors of English literature at two city universities. The only men in their lives continued to be, Wordsworth, Coleridge, Shelley, Blake, and Keats, flitting between them, at will, as the first flirtations of their adolescent flutters.

Both shared publication successes. May's collection of poems titled *Rain in May* was an autobiographical explosion — it rose to a bestseller in the first week. June wrote her sonnets, *Mother, Our Nature* which received academic accolades from Women Poets' Associations around the world. She had an unending list of requests to speak at writers' festivals. Her compositions revealed that poverty and injustice need not be deterrents in the quagmire of a life.

With local, national, and international literary tours, their social circle grew among like-minded souls. The emotional connection to their work attracted a diverse crowd into their fold. They were selective in who they drew in, the past lingered, just beneath the skin, fear and pain, a misguided word away.

YEARS LATER, in their mid-forties, they abandoned their professorships for a new life in the central west, creating their own Romanticist village retreat.

They started with the first thatched-roof cottage, *Lakes Leisure*, growing to six cottages within three years. Laid out in a circle — *Lakes Leisure, Grassmere House, Cotswold Cottage, Cumbria Comfort, Prelude Palace* — a living dream.

With their own stylized slice of heaven, literary minds gathered for writing solitude, inspiration or a Romantic era, themed wedding.

On the official opening day of the Central West Romantic Writer's Retreat, they arranged a grand party, catered food arrived in abundance, costumes of the period for hire, poetry recitals, and brilliant conversations on their poetic heroes — an imagined vision, now their reality.

Scores of people, in private cars, and hired coaches appeared, ready for a Romantic fest. Some arrived on horseback to this self-styled Cotswolds down under.

As the crowd settled to listen to May's keynote address, it was a brilliant, clear-skied afternoon, then a deluge arrived with no forewarning — a visitation to their Romantic recreated world, announcing the presence of the Mighty Being.

May looked up at the smiling sea of faces

'What can I say? When you live your life with passion, your muse comes in search of you. All our Mighty Beings are here with us today!'

The next spiritual chapter of their lives had begun.

In our angst and joy we are one under the sky of humanity
—Mala Naidoo

DID YOU ENJOY THE STORIES?

If you've enjoyed reading, *Life's Seasons - A Collection of Short Stories*, please leave an honest review to help other readers decide if they might like to read my books. This will help me to write more.

With Gratitude,

Mala Naidoo
www.malanaidoo.com